DARK
EHTER

JAVON BATES

National Sexual Assault Hotline
Hours: Available 24 hours Learn more
1-800-656-4673.

What are the six main categories of rape?
Types of Rape: The Different Forms of Rape
Diminished Capacity Rape. The type of rape known as diminished capacity rape is committed when one person forces sexual penetration on another person who cannot consent to the sex act. ...
Age-Related Rape. ...
Incest. ...
Partner Rape. ...
Acquaintance Rape. ...
Aggravated Rape. ...

The National Women's Study produced dramatic confirmation of the mental health impact of rape. The study determined comparative rates of several mental health problems among rape victims and non-victims. The study ascertained whether rape victims were more likely than non-victims to experience these devastating mental health problems. Posttraumatic Stress Disorder.

The first mental health problem examined was posttraumatic stress disorder (PTSD), an extremely debilitating disorder occurring after a highly disturbing traumatic event, such as military combat or violent crime.

Substance Abuse

There was substantial evidence that rape victims had higher rates than non-victims of drug and alcohol consumption and a greater likelihood of having drug and alcohol-related problems. Compared to women who had never been crime victims, rape victims with RR-PTSD

Sexual violence in the U.S.

One in five women and one in 71 men will be raped
at some point in their lives

46.4% lesbians, 74.9% bisexual women and 43.3%
heterosexual women reported sexual violence other
than rape during their lifetimes

While 40.2% gay
men, 47.4% bisexual men and 20.8% heterosexual
men reported sexual violence other than rape during
their lifetimes.

Nearly one in 10 women has been raped by an
intimate partner in her lifetime, including completed
forced penetration, attempted forced penetration
or alcohol/drug-facilitated completed penetration.

Approximately one in 45 men has been made to
penetrate an intimate partner during his lifetime.

91% of the victims of rape and sexual assault are
female, and 9% are male

In eight out of 10 cases of rape, the victim knew the
person who sexually assaulted them

8% of rapes occur while the victim is at work

For more information about "DARK ETHER" go to
tegmedia.org or tegmedia1@gmail.com

CONTENTS

DARK ETHER: THE CASE OF EMILY BAKER

It was about 8:47pm when Larry checked his watch. They had made good time coming in from Colorado at this rate. Touchdown had almost been at the exact estimated time, and their car had been waiting at the airport, just as they had left it. In a few minutes, they would be home and he counted on being sound asleep before the next hour was out. That ought to give him enough time to rest and recover before heading to the firm the next day, he thought. Larry thrummed his fingers on the wheel as he drove on through the night. They hadn't done badly at all.

Katherine Baker knew from the self-satisfied thrum of Larry's fingers on the wheel, that the reunion and convention were well behind him. He would go from here on, through the motions of his life, never once deigning to hit any of the old boys up, at least until whenever they decided once again to have a class reunion. Or one odd day, he would be scrolling through the contact list on his phone and that would be it. He wouldn't exactly call; those calls ended up being weird and about nothing, he would often say. Rather, he'd stare at the contact for a few seconds, smiling in reminiscence of what had once been, and then he would scroll right on.

Things were much different for Katherine, of course. She was still irked by the fact that Nelson had her mixed with Lydia for the entirety of the reunion and always wound up referencing weird incidents Katherine had absolutely no memory of, despite the amazing times they had had back in the day. Then there had been Jacqueline looking at least thirty pounds overweight and ugly in the dress she had chosen to wear to the dinner party. Katherine couldn't help feeling a sense of delight and fulfillment at the looks of horror and barely hidden disgust which were constantly fired in her direction. But that had only been in the beginning.

Somehow, in all the intervening years, Jacqueline the Princess had learnt to be more relatable, not so stuck on her high horse, and fairly funny, that she soon had the entire assembly drawn and attentive to her with her jokes and recollections. Everyone except Katherine, of course. She tried very hard to convince herself that her being so put off by Jacqueline had everything to do with the fact that her jokes were silly and lame and had nothing to do with the fact that Jacqueline had stolen her prom date and ended up becoming the Prom Queen while at it. Things just seemed to always work for girls like her, even when they were fat and ugly.

Katherine sometimes wished she could be more like Larry. She didn't want to have to worry and lose sleep over what happened in the lives of folks she hadn't seen for over two decades. It wasn't like her life was that bad. While getting with Larry hadn't been the whirlwind romance of the century, it had been respectful and quite beneficial. He had grown from the shy overly sensitive nerd she had known in high school, to a quite capable man who was vice president of a fortune five hundred company.

She didn't think there was any other woman to worry about. They had their daughter, Emily, who was waiting for them at home. That her life wasn't perfect was only because of the sentiment that nothing ever was. Hers was a solid world she didn't see anyone shaking or even breaking. She straightened up in her seat, worked up a smile, reached over, and squeezed Larry's thigh. He glanced over and smiled in return. Everything was just right.

Miles away lay the spacious grounds of their seven-acre estate property. Their house was the fourteen roomed mansion which served as its gem. Emily was in the study, lying on her back right atop the desk, and her the flash of her phone's camera winked as she took yet another picture.

"There you go, you son of a bitch," she said, voicing the very caption her thumbs typed out on the picture. "You best treat 'em titties right."

She clicked send on the picture and adjusted her blouse so her surprisingly well-formed breasts slid back within its folds. Her parents had texted as soon as their plane landed and would be home any minute now. Ordinarily, she wouldn't be doing this in here. But Jerold had asked that the pictures be kinky this time, and the study was one of her favorite places. She sat up to head out of the room to get properly prepared for her parents' return. Then, as an afterthought, she lifted the hem of her skirt, tugged her panties aside, and her camera winked again.

The door of the study clicked shut behind her. Emily was feeling very sleepy. She thought a warm shower would enliven her enough to hug her mum and dad when they came in, after which she could hit the bed. That seemed like just the thing to do, she decided, trailing her hand on the banister as she went up the stairs. Emily did not see the figure standing in the shadows of the kitchen doorway, watching her.

Katherine's stomach grumbled. "Owwf."
"What's that?" Larry said, chuckling. "Hungry so soon?"
"Nah, the other," Katherine said, adjusting uncomfortably in her seat. "I really need to use the loo."
"Right. Mama's about to make a big mess."
"Step on it, Larry," Katherine said, her seatbelt the only thing keeping her from doubling over.
"Okay, okay, captain. Yeesh," Larry said. He pushed down on the accelerator.

Emily would later swear she had shut the door of her bedroom. She was standing in the middle of her room as she tugged her blouse off over her head. Her breasts were two firm bouncy mounds with nipples that pointed a little too arrogantly even on the full-length mirror as Emily observed herself. She planted her feet squarely on the floor, took a deep breath, and bent over double to kiss her knees. She didn't get that far.

Right behind her as she dropped, reflected on the mirror, was the image an odd-looking man standing in the middle of her open doorway. Emily froze. But only for one second. She screamed and the man lunged at her.

The man must have flown, because he seemed to have covered the fifteen-foot space between them in the twinkle of an eye as he pressed himself against her behind. Emily saw, even as she struggled to break away from him, that his hands were coming up to her face. She turned instinctively aside and felt something flat, smooth yet powdery, press against the side of her face. She could not see the dark red smudge which had just about taken over that side of her face, but a sharp intake of breath filled her lungs with an overpoweringly cloying smell which shot all the way up into her head.

There was a moment of paralyzing disorientation during which the man's arms slid around her underarms and hoisted her limp form off her feet. The room spun around her, and then it was the ceiling which listed and swirled when he dropped her on the bed. She was staring into the face of a masked man.

That his mask was a pattern of eccentric circles which shifted with every movement of his, only served to further the notion that this was a dream. A dream in which he held a pair of scissors over her head. "Well, well," he said in a drawn-out smoky hiss of a voice. "These are some mighty fine tits."

His free hand traced the undersides and outlines of her breasts. "Now, to see what waits on the downside."
Emily was a dazed, paralyzed wreck as the man's scissors descended slowly to press the coldness of its steel against her lower belly, before sliding over skirt down to the very end.

The scrich-schrich of shredding fabric filled her ears as the man sliced her skirt open through the middle. All that was left now was the awareness that she was totally exposed to the man's imperceptible gaze but for the sheer slip of her panties, and that even that would soon give way in the face of his nifty tool.

It was the sound of a car roaring ever closer in the distance which told Emily that she wasn't entirely helpless. Those were her parents coming, and if she could just delay him somewhat for a little bit, perhaps all would be right. Through the fog of whatever she had been drugged with, Emily found that with every fresh breath that she took, her head wasn't so woozy, and she was gaining control of most of her senses. With that came a few lessons in gymnastics from cheerleading practice.

"Pubes," the man said in that smoky voice which had gone husky. "I love the look of your pubes."

His free hand reached down and grabbed the edge of her panties. Just then, Emily felt the weight of him shift ever so slightly off her legs. One quick pull, brought both her knees up to her chest, knocking his hand off her undies.

Then she drove both her feet hard into the man's face. The force of it propelled her off the bed in a somersault, and Emily was finally standing free on the side of it, catching her breath. The man's hand grabbed the sheets from the other side over which he had tumbled, and Emily realized she wasn't out of harm's way yet. She fled.

"Heelllllp!" she screamed as she raced out her bedroom and down the stairs. She heard the man's heavy footfalls pounding behind her and that only spurred her on her flight. "Helllppp!"

The heavy oak door slid wide open as she got to the foot of the stairs, and her parents walked into the house. Emily crashed right into her mother, too much in a hysterical fit to do anything but point upstairs behind her.

"What happened? What's going—" Larry was in the middle of saying when he heard the smash of glass somewhere upstairs. Then he was racing up the stairs.

"Come on, Emily, tell me what—" Katherine said pulling her daughter aside. She grabbed Emily's face to steady her and saw the thick moistened redness on the side of her daughter's face. Blood. Katherine screamed.

It's Dark Ether

The flash of the camera brought Detective Jessica Taylor back to the present. It wasn't blood, she thought, staring at the red smudges all around the bedroom. It was something else. Something she was very familiar with. She heard the heavy-soled footfalls as a man entered the room and came to stand beside her. Her partner, Detective James Reeves.

"It's him, right?" he said in a raspy voice.
"Yep," Jessica said, nodding. "It's him alright."
There was another camera flash and Jessica turned to the only other person in the bedroom with them. He was fiddling with the lens on his camera, and the tag on his white coveralls identified him as a forensic photographer.

"Hi there, think you've got enough pictures?" she said.
He looked up at her as if startled out of his concentration. "Just a few more."
"Okay then. Let's wrap up as soon as possible," she said, walking out of the bedroom with her partner following hard behind her. She had everything she needed.

The golden sheen of the Ohio sun filled the living room as the detectives came down the stairs. They had been reasonably late to the party, and the rest of the officers had practically cleared out. They hadn't been the first point of call when the case was first reported. Initially thought to be a simple home invasion when the 911 call came in, the seriousness of the matter wasn't fully appreciated until a couple of officers had shown up and questioned the young girl.

Emily, on what had transpired. That was last night.
"I can't tell you enough, but you were really lucky last night. And brave," Jessica said as they marched up to the family huddled together on the couch in the living room. She stood before them, arms akimbo. "The man who came here last night is a sicko. And very dangerous."
"Okay, I know I've asked this before, but I just can't wrap my head around it," the girl's father, Larry Baker, said leaning forward. "You

mean to tell me he's been doing this for a while? How come we haven't heard about him? And why haven't you caught him yet."
"It's actually been reported a couple of times," James told him. "Just not with the full picture. We sometimes leave out certain details to keep cases like this properly distinguished and prevent against copycats."

"You sound like he was a serial killer," Emily said, looking up at the detectives, confused.
"Well, he is a serial rapist. And the red stuff from yesterday is part of his unique signature. That part, we left out of the news," Jessica told her. "We believe he stalks his victims for days, possibly weeks, until he finds an opening. The red stuff? Dark ether. That's what he uses to sedate his victims. You're lucky he didn't really get that stuff over your face properly."

"You mean he's probably been hanging around the house?" Emily pulled her knees up off the floor under her chin. Her mother rubbed her gently on the back.
"What if he comes back?" Larry asked.

"Your daughter is the first failed attempt of his and is thus unprecedented. We can't make any real predictions, but I don't think you have anything to fear about a second attack," James said. "However, I will advise taking a trip to cool off your head if that will make you feel safe."
"Are you suggesting that we flee?" Katherine fired. "This is our home. How about you just do your job?"

"Yes, Mrs. Baker. That is precisely what we intend to do," James said. Jessica stood there watching Emily who had shrunken so much between her parents like a ball of a child. There was yet another thing unprecedented about this case. Nine known cases in and the man they had codenamed Dark Ether was yet to break character on any ground. The sedative, the voice, the mask, everything fit properly into his MO. Was he intending to branch out now or was this just a one-off incident? That would really fuck up everything they thought they knew about him. Jessica decided to ask the one question that had been bugging her since arriving at the house.

"I'm sorry, Mr. and Mrs. Baker if this seems odd, but I've just got to ask." She turned her gaze on the raven-haired kid. "Emily, have you ever been blonde before?"

They slid out the house into the golden sun. There were two cars parked in the driveway beyond them, but Jessica did not quite see those. She was still mulling over what had transpired so far. "From out of the blues, a brunette."

James stuck a cigarette in between his lips and set a lighter to it. He took in a deep breath and exhaled a thick plume of smoke. "So, where do we go from here?"
"Back to the drawing board, I guess," Jessica said with a sigh. "Or we wait for his next attempt, see if there's a new pattern forming."
The door clicked open behind them, there were a few steps, and then it slammed shut. The detectives turned to the photographer coming up behind them.

"Well, you certainly took your time in there," James said, breathing smoke.
"You know the job," the man said, approaching Jessica. "Every square inch, every tile scoured. You never know where the clues might be hiding."
Jessica smiled as he bridged the gap between them and kissed her lightly on the lips. Franklin Taylor. Her boyish looking, curly haired nerd of a husband. He tasted of the honeyed cereal she had packed him for lunch.

"How did we do?" she asked when they broke up, wiping a smudge off his collar.
"Let's just say she really caught him off guard," Frank said. "He was all over the place with ether. Smudges here and there. I really hoped to get some blood at the bathroom window he broke in his escape, but no luck there. Careful as ever."
"Eh. One of these days, his luck will run out," Jessica said.
"How about a little bit of space between you two?" James said. "Am I the only one who thinks this a bit inappropriate that you two be doing that here, after what just happened?"

"Careful, James," Jessica said, smiling. "Jealousy brings forth bad fruits."

There was a vibration between them and the lovers immediately parted ways as Frank reached into his pocket. He took one look at his phone and gasped.

"Oh, shit. I forgot," he said, hurrying a few steps away from Jessica. "What?"

"Matthew. He's getting out today," he said. "I was supposed to pick him up from the hospital."

"What?! How could you forget something so—what are you waiting for? Go, go, go. I'll fix shit up at the house," Jessica told him, even as her heart began to pound.

"Thank you, thank you, thank you very much," he yelled as he raced down the steps to his car. "I love you."

"Go," Jessica told him.

It was so like Frank to forget things like this, she thought as he raced all the way down to his car. Thankfully, that was where his vices ended.

The Thing About Kids

Jessica's heart was a booming cannon when the door to her house slid open and she found herself face to face with a teenager who was so definitely Frank's son. The resemblance was so uncanny and the realization that she would never be able to birth someone as similar or anyone at all sent a large lump down her throat that she forgot to scream—

"Welcome hoooome!" Imelda screamed, saving the moment. Imelda was her janitor and Jessica found herself stretching an arm towards the other woman to lean on her for support before catching herself. She smiled at the mini Frank, stretching her arm out to him instead.

"Hello there, Matthew," she said. "Welcome home." For his part, the small skinny boy of thirteen, with a head full of dark curly locks that reminded Jessica of the treachery of genes, just stood there in the doorway, staring at them. Jessica saw him take in the living room, running over the furniture and the decorations that had been put up on his behalf, without betraying a single emotion on his face.

That was something in that self-possession, which was reminiscent of the way his father, Frank, sometimes got lost in his own head, mulling over this or that fact, or the angle of that item in this or that photograph. Both were men very capable of existing solidly and sufficiently, without regards or leanings to the rest of the world.

A quality which had endeared Jessica to Frank after her marriage to her ex-husband whose attachment and need for the children she had been so incapable of having had almost driven her to such despairing depths. She had felt enough guilt about it all and didn't need him piling on some more. Frank was just the exact opposite. Sometimes too much, and Jessica believed she was seeing just how much in the face of his teenage son.

Frank poked his head through the doorway behind Matthew with a wide gleaming yet bashful smile as he rapped his knuckles on the door.

"Greetings, Earthlings. We come in peace," he said.
Jessica couldn't help the smile which rose to her face at his goofiness.
"Come in here you two."
"Alright," he sang as he nudged Matthew further into the house. "Go on in, Matthew. This is home now."

He strolled past the young man, bearing a large rucksack. He gave Jessica a kiss on the cheek and stood between her and Imelda.
"This is Imelda. She's the help," he said. "And this, this is Jessica. You've met. She's my wife and, I hope, your mother."
As if spurred on by the force of three adults staring down at him, daring him to reject them, Matthew took his first three steps further into the house.

They were very leaden ones, and Jessica thought that he would sink into the ground through the floorboards. Jessica took a couple of steps towards him, bridging the gap between them, and leaned down so their faces were level.

"Hello, young man. Nice to finally meet you properly," she said. "I'm Jessica, like your bigheaded daddy over there says. I know that things seem a little weird, but I'm willing to walk at your pace. You don't have to call me mum or anything, if you don't want. But I hope very much that we could both be friends."

The young man held her gaze solidly with his expressionless eyes. The air hung tensely between them that it was all she could do to sneak in a few breaths. Finally, he blinked.
"Can I be shown to my room now?" he said, breaking the trance but leaving the tension just as thick.

"Oh, okay then," she said, straightening up.
"Alright, Sir Matthew," Imelda said, stretching her thick fleshed arm to him. "I'll take you in."
Frank's eyebrows were arched in an embarrassed manner, and he

17

squeezed his skinny shoulders apologetically as he turned to follow Imelda and Matthew inside with the rucksack. They left Jessica alone in the living room, trying to wrap her head around the import of what had just happened. Her arms wrapped themselves protectively around her midriff, a mirror of him too as he had been through it all. And what was that he had been clutching to his chest the entire time? Had that been a Bible?

The honk-honk of cars edging through traffic on Euclid Avenue filled the air as Jessica made her way through the parking lot. Yet the click-clack-click-clack of her soles as she walked on was all the external sound she was conscious of as she strolled. She had come here for news. Whether it was good or bad would determine the course of her life for the nearest future.

Jessica remembered this was weeks before news of Dark Ether's first victim broke. She remembered that she had left the precinct prior to her break time and much earlier than the Chief would approve, and that she hadn't told anyone either where she was headed. But the question which had been on her mind for some long years now demanded an answer, and that was what she was here for.

The Lyndfarb Jane building had been there for twenty-five years by that point. Catering solely to the reproductive and sexual concerns of women, Jessica believed if there was either an answer or a solution to be got on her issue, and as anonymously as possible, it would be here, within these halls. For an organization that had been the offshoot of quite feministic aspirations, Jessica was shocked to find the hallways and doors painted with the stereotypically female pink. Apparently, there were those who thought that shying away from the recognized symbols of femininity was an inadvertent confession that one thought there was something wrong with being a woman.

Her appointment had been booked three days prior to her visit and she had phoned ahead before hitting the road, so she didn't have to wait for long before being ushered into the doctor's office.

"Hi, there," he said to her. "Do sit down."

The plaque on his desk identified him as Steve Cohen. This was her first time coming here and she had never met the man before. Jessica wondered therefore if it was the policy of the organization to employ eye candy doctors with the aim of pandering to the female gaze that was so forcefully neglected outside.

Steve was a fine man, distractingly handsome. Admitting she had a problem to such a pretty man was definitely going to be a problem. She took her seat.

"So, what seems to be the problem Ms…" he paused to check her file.

"O'Hara," she told him. "Jessica O'Hara."

"Yes. Jessica O'Hara," he said with a smile that was both meant to be professional and charming as well. "How may we help you?"

"Babies," Jessica said. "My husband and I have been trying for a couple of years to no avail. We'd like to have babies."

Jessica saw a flicker in his eyes, and an image flashed in her mind. What she believed he saw.

She on the desk, her legs splayed wide; him between them, ramming to his heart's content.

"May I ask then why your husband isn't here with you?" he said.

The detective saw with the slight flare of his nostrils, that this doctor did not approve at all of the situation.

"He doesn't know about this appointment," she said. "I uh… I lived somewhat roughly as a teenager and in my early twenties. And uhh…"

Her voice trailed off, leaving him to finish the statement for her.

"You suspect that something might be the matter with you, after all," the doctor said.

Jessica nodded and blinked to stop the tears of embarrassment currently fogging her vision.

"Alright then. Step over here let's see what we can learn," he said, gesturing at the screened off section of the office.
The hysterosalpingography and ovarian reserve tests which followed didn't take long and proved precisely what Jessica had known all along.

An older case of Chlamydia had fucked her up royally. Not wanting to lead him on any further when there was no hope in sight, she had quickly relayed the ugly news to her husband, Lewin. Of course, once the immediate shock and storm was over, he kidded himself that they could somehow work their way through it. It didn't take long before he was cheating because their marriage was foundering, and he needed some sort of validation.

The divorce had followed quickly and without fuss. Jessica poured herself into her work, trying to catch Dark Ether who was then beginning to be a serious menace. She didn't forget to get a few rounds with the good Doctor, either. Some things were just the natural order of things.

No Big Deal

"It was quite a hectic drive too," Frank said. "He most definitely didn't mean anything by it. At least, not in the way that adults generally mean such things."
"I know. I don't think he meant anything by it, either," Jessica said as she did a touch up of her mascara.

"Yeah, I guessed that. It's just, that was also quite awkward. You don't know how many times I felt like jumping in to salvage the situation somewhat. But then, I thought you were the champ. Nothing you can't handle. And you did well in my opinion actually."
"Okay, come on, Babe.

You don't have to try to placate or patronize me," Jessica said, turning to hold him by the collar, however awkwardly with mascara bottle and brush in either hand. "It was indeed an awkward moment and could have gone better, but it also really could have been much worse. I wasn't expecting our first time meeting each other to be all sunshine and rainbows. So yes, I'm fine. And I think we will be fine too. Just chill, my love. Okay?"

She gave him a kiss on the lips. Frank smiled and she smiled back. Then she turned to face the mirror.
They were in the bathroom, a flaming orange affair, with a circular mirror into which they stared as Jessica applied mascara the shade of her black little dress. Frank for his part was busy trying to magic the strap around his neck into a bow tie fitting of the tuxedo which lay waiting on the bed in the bedroom.

He hoped to God that the party to which they were headed would be worth all this stress.
"One thing did bug me, though," Jessica said as she brushed yet another powder Frank couldn't recognize or name into the underside of her eyes. "You didn't tell me Phoebe was religious."
"Religious?" Frank said, snorting. "Where on earth did you get that idea?"

"I don't know. Matthew had what I believe was a Bible with him. With the way he held on to it, I figured it was something very precious. Like if he got it from his mum. You know that sort of thing."

"Oh, no, no. Not at all," Frank said, getting back to work on his tie with a smile. "The hospital—"

"What? They incorporated religious instruction into the program? What are they, mission owned? Did you consent to all that?"

"No. Not that," Frank said, chuckling as he faced his suddenly upset wife. "Matthew just—he made a friend in there. An older one. Got the Bible as a parting gift. I'm guessing it's the next best thing to comfort and connection he's got."

"Oh, okay then." Jessica turned to survey her work in the mirror, turning sideways, one way then the other. She looked good.
She turned to Frank and pulled him to her by the collar. Then she went to work on the bowtie. This was one of those instances when Frank really did seem ever lost and from which she was always on hand to bail him. Sometimes, it seemed damned near incredible that her near genius husband really did find himself incapacitated in the face of such simplicities.

"Look at you being all Wifely, Mrs. Taylor," Frank said. His arms snaked around her to hold sizable portions of her ample ass. "And might I interpret your current woody as a symbol of your appreciation?"

"You bet." Frank's head drew closer to hers and they kissed.
He turned to look at himself in the mirror. The tie was just perfect and did a whole lot to solidify his mushy baby boy looks. They were ready to face the world now.
"One thing, Jess," Frank said. "Nobody can know Matthew was in the psych ward."

One Hell of a Speech

The Cross continental hotel had been around since the 30's. Part of its long story of achievements and one of which it was most proud, was the fact that it had played host to Franklin D. Roosevelt during the early days of his Presidential Campaign. Jessica didn't think that anything to be particularly awed by, considering that the hotel had played host to a wide range of celebrities and politicians through the decades. Still, you did not tell another person which moments to hold dear as precious gems.

That night, the hotel's Cherub Hall was packed full to the brim. There were commissioners of police, both old as well as the incumbent. There were lawyers who had severed as counterparts to the police from the office of the district attorney. Journalists and news bloggers who did not always see eye to eye with the force members. There were the civilians who formed part of the retinue of family and friends, and there were the not-so civilians who had come as emissaries and delegates from politicians in different offices. And it was all on account of Police Chief Fenwick.

It was rumored around in certain circles that Chief Fenwick had risen through the ranks by being the go-to service boy of the rich and the powerful in manners that weren't so pristine. Certain key evidences disappearing because someone was so conveniently negligent, certain people being fingered for certain crimes in the moments when they stepped on the toes of someone very powerful.

These allegations and suspicions flowed consistently from the bloggers and other press agents, yet the man continued to ascend the ladder of success, seemingly protected from it all, almost in the very same manner as alleged by the press in the first place. Of course, the most of Fenwick's loyalist and subordinates disbelieved and discountenanced such ideas wherever they ran into them. Fenwick was simply shrewd and hardworking. And good luck sometimes seemed to only shine on specific people.

Detective Jessica Taylor was one of such loyalists, and she beamed with pride as she stood there beside her husband, Franklin Taylor, as the Police Chief jogged up the podium to address the crowd that had gathered to celebrate on this event of retirement. Chief Fenwick had virtually guided her on the path of her own career. It was he who had first suggested that she would do remarkably well if she ever made detective. A few more years on, she might have very well been one of those sufficiently placed to be his successor. Sometimes, however, luck did run out, and in this instance, Chief Fenwick's retirement had come up much earlier than anticipated.

The audience applauded and cheered, roaring their support and best wishes as Chief Fenwick looked this way and that, waving to his friends, with a smile that only ever came from the most dignified and handsome of Hollywood celebrities. He was Richard Gere. Only slightly fatter.

"Alright, alright, you people. Sit down so I can get this speech started and get out of here," Fenwick said, smiling even as he said it.
"We love you, Fenny," someone said from the crowd.
"Your wife heard that," he said, and the crowd roared with laughter. Finally and eventually, they did sit down, and the applause and cheers subsided.

Fenwick stood there still, smiling a forlorn smile as his eyes roved over the crowd.
"Thirty-four years," he said. He let a couple of heartbeats pass over those words, before he continued. "I look at all of you, and I think thirty-four years. What a marvelous treasure. You know, I almost didn't make it as a police officer? Most of you don't know this, but I was born a little short sighted."

Of course, everybody knew it, Jessica thought. There was hardly an event and hardly a speech where he didn't restate this fact.
"I was born a little short sighted, and the more that I grew, the clearer it became that I would go blind soon and that would be the end of the matter. By the time I was a teenager, and not in the way that kids sometimes parrot other people with their dreams and aspirations, when I started telling folks that I wanted to be a police

officer, they would laugh at me. I became something of a caricature of the detective peering so intently at the evidence, not because I was trying to solve anything, but because I simply couldn't see. I pushed on nonetheless, decided to join the academy. At our certification exams, I was one of the worst graduating students.

But here we are today, with the help of hardwork, dedication and a few eye-drops, outgoing Chief of police."
The audience roared, standing up to applaud and cheer for a few moments until Fenwick put out his hand for peace. Slowly, they took their seats again.

"Robbers and petty-thieves, corporate criminals, murderers and would-be killers, rapists; these were brought to book by my office, through the hard work of the most efficient members of the police force, and there was no wish greater than to serve the needs of the general public. So, I ask, is there any way in which I have failed you? I'll answer that. I'll indict myself personally by saying, inasmuch as we weren't our best at all times, inasmuch as we weren't perfect upon every given instance it was required of us, we have failed you. Dark Ether."

There was a pause. Then came the slight and fast spreading murmur as people realized and recognized the name that had just been mentioned. "If there has been any failure I take most personally and painfully, it's been that of our failure to apprehend the criminal known as Dark Ether. In the hours between eight and nine pm last night, it was reported that a girl had just been attacked and nearly raped in what seemed to be a home invasion.

A subsequent investigation would later reveal that rather than a burglary or a home invasion, this was in fact, the serial rapist, Dark Ether, at his worst again. Thanks to God and Providence, he was unsuccessful. "Had he succeeded, this would have made it the tenth girl to suffer his defilement and corruption. The substance with which he sedates his victims, the dark ether, is a substance known to be highly addictive."

Jessica felt her head go woolen at that, so much so, she placed one of her arms on Frank's thigh to steady herself. That was the crazy about memory. It sometimes caused physical reactions to the event remembered.

"While there are no known physical symptoms to withdrawal, I want you to imagine his victims getting hooked to the drug that they find themselves returning every time to the very tool of their own oppression and victimization. I have a daughter. Two, actually. One of them is married. But while it is easy to presume, she is therefore safe from the Ether's eyes, we have reason to suspect that Dark Ether doesn't discriminate as much as we thought.

"So, I have two daughters, and I've often found myself in the wake of one of the Ether's attacks, sitting in the dark, wondering what I would do if such a terrible fate, as these other girls suffered, were visited on one of my own. I do not believe that I would exhibit the level of professionalism expected of me in the event of his eventual capture. I'm not supposed to say these things, but I'm saying them now.

I'm a civilian. Go ahead and sue me. That motherfucker touches one of mine, he had better run and hide, because castration probably would be the least of his worries if I ever did get him. I therefore want to apologize, first and foremost to the girls who were his victims, both fully and attempted, and importantly, I must apologize to their parents.

I am sorry. I am sorry that me and the officers in my department were unable to be there to save you in the moment when you needed us the most. I am truly sorry for all the agony that you all have had to pass through and are continually passing through with each new report of the Ether's most recent cases.

I retire from my position as Chief of police, primarily because I am an ailing man and no longer have the capacity to continue as such, but also because I cannot conscientiously carry on with the knowledge of this great failure I have occasioned. I have tried to do my job, but I have also failed woefully. And so, we must look to the future.

"Two detectives have been put on the case. Detectives Jessica Taylor and James Reeves; two of our department's brightest gems. I know they are both in the crowd giving me the stink eye because no one likes to be put on the spot like this. But that is precisely why I'm doing this. I believe that with the spotlight on both of them like this, they would be spurred, galvanized into closing this case and ending this menace which has plagued our society. So, yeah. Detective Taylor, Detective Reeves, you hate me, you hate me, I love you too."
The crowd chuckled uneasily.

"Let us raise our glasses then, Ladies and Gentlemen," Chief Fenwick said. "to the end of a dark and frightful era, and to the beginning of a new one. A bright and shiny chapter of our history in which the monsters and demons and bloodsuckers who plague us will be done away with and defeated. To the future."

"To the future," Jessica chorused beside her husband and the rest of the crowd. She clinked glasses with Frank, smiling, as the band went right to work with music.
"Fenwick just passed the torch, huh?" Frank said.
"Passed the torch? More like lit the pyre," Jessica said. "It's either catch the bastard tomorrow, or have the press chew our asses from here on to Uranus. Not cool at all."

"Are you going to tell him?" Frank nodded as Fenwick strolled down through the auditorium towards them, pausing occasionally to shake this or that persons, while the rest smiled on.
"Tell me you left your revolver at home, Officer," Fenwick said when he got up to them.

"Revolver? A bazooka would be more appropriate for the dagger you just stuck in my back."
"Ouch. I've never known myself to inspire such murderous sentiments," Fenwick said chuckling even as he glanced around.
"Even Reeves looks like he wants my head too."
Jessica turned in James's direction, just in time to see him look away as he took a cold stiff sip from his glass. She felt her palms go cold

suddenly at the idea that perhaps, James hadn't been looking at Fenwick at all. That probably explained the feeling of being watched that had been with her for a while now.

"Hello, Frank," Fenwick said, turning to him. "How are things at the lab?"

"Coming along just fine," Frank said. "Happy retirement, Chief."

"Thank you very much. And you, Frank, would do well to take care of the Missus right here. She's the pride and joy of our department, but she will need all the support she can get now that I'm gone."

"Hey, I'm right here, and you're talking of me like some sort of invalid," Jessica said with a playful tap on Fenwick's arm. "Also, you better stop sounding like you're dying sometime soon. You're living an eternity."

"How do I escape you then?"

All three of them chuckled. Taking a sip of her wine, Jessica turned in James's direction. He was staring right at her, and their eyes met. It was all she could do not to choke.

I Saw You Looking at Me

Moments later, Jessica was seated on the steps that led up to the Western end of the hotel. She took a lungful of her cigarette, and when she exhaled, her breath was one thick cloud of churning smoke which dissipated fast in the cool night air. The moon was one big giant ball of snow in the sky, and up ahead of her was a water fountain from which a wolf spewed forth copious amount of water as though it was sickened by his fabled ties to that celestial body. One way or the other, something ended up making you sick.

She turned her mind to the new case and pondered on its peculiarity. First was the bit of Emily being the first wealthy victim of the Dark Ether's. Was that important or merely an accident? And what about the fact of Emily's hair being black? The golden hair of his previous victims had been duly noted during the course of the investigation. It was either something of a fetish, or there had been another blonde in his history inspiring his actions. They had leaned towards the latter. But what did Emily's black hair mean? That they had been wrong after all and that his tastes had simply shifted, or that there was another woman somewhere on whom he was now fixated? If this change could occur, then perhaps some of their assumptions about him weren't all that fundamental.

Dark Ether. It had been a while, she realized as she took a long hard drag of her cigarette. Once again, she felt that slight downwards swoon hit her head as she recalled its effects. It was funny how much could over one course of event. An accident that could only be regarded as a fluke. Then suddenly, you're hooked and reeling through whirlpools of danger. She didn't know whether to be mad at Frank because it had happened at his lab, or to be grateful to him for covering up for her like a dutiful husband. All she knew was that it had opened the window to a whole new world she hoped would never come to light.

Jessica wished she could go back to much simpler times. The period in between her two marriages had been one of the freest times of her life. Even her mistakes then hadn't been mistakes, they were simply alternative choices. Lord knew there were certain choices right now that she really wished to unmake. And then there were those which left her hanging, like Matthew's presence in her house. She had been warned that he had gone through a lot, but she hadn't it was so much that he had to walk around with a Bible. And yeah, she may have told Frank that it was okay, but—

"Hi there, Detective?"
Jessica's heart gave a lurch as she turned around to find James standing a few paces away, smoking a cigarette.
"I've been getting that all evening," he continued as he took a few steps closer and sat beside her. "'Detective' mind you. Not officer or anything fancy like that. Almost like they were mocking me or something. The detective who can't detect shit."
"That might be a matter of perspective," Jessica told him.

"Oh, yeah? Chief Fenwick just set us up to take the fall for whatever goes wrong. It may have seemed like he was taking responsibility with his weepy speech up there, but what he was really doing was trying to earn sympathy. I'm an old man. I'm ashamed. See how my conscience bleeds. I nearly went blind once. People hear that and go, 'oh, he's a really good guy. Police work must have taken a toll on him.' He's out of the heat. But guess which two detectives got fingered for being in charge of the case."

"That information was out there from the moment we took it over from Dyson and Joe. We've had press briefings for crying out loud." "But not with all the heat the Chief's just directed our way," he said. "I guess we'll just have to do our jobs then. Catch the Dark Ether like we're supposed to."

"Oh, please be realistic," James snapped. "Nine cases in, the man's yet to have any slip-ups. Cases like these sometimes take decades to be resolved, other times, never. And very rarely by the same officers at the start of it."

"So you're giving up then?" Jessica fired back. "Probably because it isn't one of your own suffering the damages."
"Don't take it there now—"
"And why not?" Jessica said, glaring at him. She took a moment to bring her breathing which had spiraled out of control back to normal. "Look, Emily Baker represents the first known unsuccessful attempt of the Ether's. A slip up or not, you know it's more shit like that we need to hope and look out for to make the big break. Just hold your shit together."

Jessica turned to find that James was smiling at her. "What?" she said. "You really would make a great Police Chief," he said. She couldn't help the smile which came to her face. So, she turned to stare at the moon, with a slow drag of her cigarette.

"What do you think of this A-hole new Chief getting transferred here? Braxton," James took a puff of his smoke. "Fucker didn't even have the courtesy of showing up at the party."
"I don't know," Jessica said with a shrug.

"If he's been set up to take Fenwick's place by the powers that be, I'm guessing he's just as good a politician. It would be wise to have him like you." "Hmm," he said, mulling over her words. Finally, he looked up. "So, how are you?"

"How am I?" Jessica said, slightly confused. "I'm fine. I'm good."
"I meant, how are you?" James said, fixing her a solid stare. "Feeling any withdrawal symptoms?"

Right. Finally, it was out. The real reason behind all this sudden awkwardness. Beside her husband, Frank, this was the only other person who knew she used the substance, Dark Ether. Had used the substance. After incident at Frank's lab, she had found herself chasing more and more of the ether's euphoric high, and she hadn't been very good at hiding it. At least, not to those closest to her.
"I'm good. I'm great. You've got nothing to worry about," she said. "What about you? How are you holding up? Are you good?"
"Am I good?" he snorted. "Why are you out here, Jessica?"
"Why am I—what—what do you mean?" she said.

James sighed like a tired old man. "Where's your husband, Frank?"
"Frank's up inside. Last I saw him, he was talking with Fenw—"
James moved in quick and pressed his cold lips up against Jessica's.
"Woah, woah, woah," she said as she jumped up straight, looking to see if there was anybody around who saw. "What was that about?"
"Come on now," James said as he rose to his feet. "Let's cut it all out now. The drama, the tricks, the mind games. It's childish and unnecessary."

"Childish and unnecessary? What the fuck are you talking about?" she said, taking a few steps backwards.
"You knew what you wanted when you came out here," James said, trying to close the distance between them. "You knew exactly whom you were waiting for. So can we just—"

"I came out to steal a smoke, what the hell are you on about?"
"I tried to stay away, 'dammit," James said. "I tried not to approach you no matter how much it hurt. But I couldn't ignore the signs anymore. You want this, Jess. Just as much as I—"
"What signs are you—hold it, James," Jessica said, realizing they were somewhat in the shadows now and he had her cornered. "If you take another step forward, I'll be forced to hurt you, and not just that. I'm hitting your ass with a lawsuit."

"Oh, fuck me," James said, chuckling as he ran his hand through his hair. "This is crazy." There was a moment's pause. And then he launched. Jessica found herself staggering backwards from the force of his kiss as he tried to force her lips open while his hands roamed about for a feel of her hip and breast.

She buckled a bit before finding her feet. She dug her heels in and sent a solid knee straight into James's crotch. He groaned with a burst of breath into Jessica's mouth, but just at the same time, she was grabbing his shoulders. Putting her back to it, she hurled him aside away from her, and just as he went staggering by, she put out a foot to trip him. There was no breaking his fall as James landed sideways on the steps, groaning.

Jessica was heaving as she watched him writhing on the floor. She thought of saying something mean to him. She turned and ran instead. She was running still as she broke in through the halls of the hotel and crashed right into her husband.

"Hey, hey, there. What's up? What's the matter with you?" he said, looking down at her with concern in his eyes as he tried to stifle the mirth from whatever joke he had been listening to.
"It was—it was—nothing," Jessica said, straightening up against him. "I just had to catch my breath."

The Gilliam Escalation

He was heaving, his nostrils flared, as he watched her through the window. She was seated in the living room, flipping through TV channels with a remote in one hand, while the other held her phone into which she glanced from time to time. Her name was Meredith Gilliam, he had learnt, and she was all alone. What did she know?

Could she sense how much danger was about to befall her? He took another look at those inky black locks on her head. He felt his nostrils flare once again, and melted away from the window.

Cunts. They were cunts, every single one of them. They were cunts, and they weren't worth shit. Not unless you used them for manure, and then, they were worth just about the same. Heck, they all smelled the same.

He made his way around the house to the back porch. Her dog, Fifi—going by her collar, was currently sound asleep on the wooden floor. That was on account of the tasty treat he had lured her out with. Nothing like a jolly snack laced with sedatives to send you well on your way.

He got to her back door. The key to being successful at what he did was to know precisely what you had to do beforehand. That took preparation and precision. For instance, there was her back door. Unless she was practically deafened by loud music, chances were she would definitely hear her back door slide open. Good thing he had a canister of lube with him.

He squirted some into both hinges, then just in case the door was imperfectly balanced to rest its weight on the ground, he squirted some underneath as well. Then squatting, he went to work with his lock picking tools.

Everything he did, he did in between heartbeats. There was always a chance of some silly neighbor looking out their windows, spotting you and dialing 911. As such, you had to always look like you belonged precisely where you were and there was no trouble whatsoever. Calmness and speed were thus very necessary for success. There would be time for excitement and making a mess afterwards.

The door slid open full thirteen seconds after he went to work on it. He slid into the house, quietly like a wraith, and shut the door just as quietly behind him. He was in her kitchen and the whole place reeked of stale and rotting food. The intruder strolled over to the sink and plugged the drain. He turned the taps on low, then he slid behind the door to the hallway. All he had to do now was wait.

Breathing was one of the most underrated things in human history. There wasn't any problem which could not be solved if all you did was pause and take a few deep breaths. There was nothing which worked best at clearing your mind and centering you like breathing slowly and consciously.

As he stood there behind the door, breathing slowly, he told himself that this was probably just bullshit sold by lots of bullshit peddlers, but which he currently needed to pass the time.

One minute. Two minutes. Three. The human mind wasn't really built for inertia. We've been conditioned to take action. For even the most indolent, unless when asleep, there's always something to do, even if that meant flipping through multiple web pages on the internet.

The urge to act, no matter how ill advised, increased most exponentially in the face of a problem. The intruder couldn't deny that standing there behind the door, watching the sink fill up and spill over got to him as much as it was intended to get to the occupant in the living room. He breathed some more.

Finally, he heard some movement in the living room. The sounds emanating from the TV went low, no doubt turned down for a proper listen.

"Jesus, fuck!" the girl exploded.

Meredith Gilliam. Here she came, the man thought, his heart pounding in increased palpitations as he pulled his mask down over his face and became the Dark Ether.

"You have got to be kidding— "

Three short quick steps bridged the distance between them as the Dark Ether came behind her and clamped a hankie over her nostrils and mouth.

"Breathe," he told her as she squealed into his palm and tried to struggle away from him. He held her solidly to himself, pressed his palms firmly over her face even long after she had gone limp.

He had neither forgotten nor forgiven what happened with the last. Finally, he let his palms off her face and set her down on the bare floor. The water from the taps had just about gotten to the lip of the sink, so he turned them off and unplugged it. Only then did he allow himself a proper look at his victim as she lay there sprawled on the floor. His penis gave a lurch in his pants.

Whistling a tune, he turned to her knife rack and picked one out. Pushing her feet apart with his legs, he knelt between them. He took a handful of her shirt, slid the knife under it, and in three sharp moves, slit it entirely open. He glanced at her full unencumbered breasts and took a lungful of breath. He turned the knife downwards, stuck it underneath the waistbands of her skirt, and in one long move, sliced it open. She had granny panties on. But even those couldn't dampen the effect of looking at her all so exposed like that before him. Stupid cunt.

Fishing rapidly in his pocket for his condom with one hand, the other unzipped his fly and fished out his throbbing penis.
"Leave no evidence behind," he muttered to himself as he slid the condom over the head of his penis. Her panties slid aside easily enough as he slid inside Meredith. He imagined them all. All the bitches, all the whores he had ever known. They were worthless. They were nothing. He had the last laugh. He would always have the last laugh.

"Bitch," he cursed as he went on with Meredith.
"Stupid cunt whore bitch," he said, looking down at her slacken face.
"Who's stupid now? Who's the weakling now? Who can't do a single thing to stop me now?"

He was panting, heaving as he spoke.
"I should fuck you up for good. I should take off my condom and splashed my seed all over your insides so you have to carry my baby as a reminder for all time. And if you ever aborted that, I'd come right back and knock you up some more.

"You're a piece of shit. All you ever were a piece of shit. Your mother, your sisters, even your soft ass dad was a piece of shit. You're nothing. Worthless. Worthless."
Meredith stirred in her drug induced sleep. She whimpered. That egged him on some more.

"Oh, you like that, don't you?" he said as he leaned in closer and increased the force of his thrusts. He sank one of his hands through the curls of her hair and pulled it backwards, angling her chin upwards. She whimpered again.

"Yeah. That's it, you bitch," he said. "That's it. You want this. You've always wanted this. I've been seeing those signs, you whore. I've been seeing them and here you are. Take it. Take what's coming to you. Here it comes."

He felt it building, the pressure ready to explode. He sped up some more and forced a fist inside his mouth to stifle his groan when he came.

He realized he hated her as he rose up off her. Lying there, so helpless, her legs spread out almost as if she were mocking him, he realized he hated her more than he had ever hated anyone. She had humiliated him. She was constantly humiliating him.

The Dark Ether picked the knife once again. As he placed the point of it just over the mound of her right breast, it occurred to him that he was just about to cross a very huge line. There was no going back from here.

He took one last breath and pushed the knife inwards with all his strength. Meredith's eyes flashed open immediately, but whatever scream had been in them quickly died down as the light faded from her eyes.

The Dark Ether sank the knife in all the way to the hilt, blood pooling around it and sliding off. Slowly, he pulled it back out again. There were fifteen more stabs to come.

A Media Circus

Jessica came out of the house, heading for the news vans and their cameras.

"Detective! Detective!" they called out to her. "What have you got for us? What can you tell us about the lady who was just murdered?" The entire street of this suburb was lined out with numerous police cars. There was an ambulance parked out, and they had wheeled in the forensic van as well. It was the whole deal, the real shindig. And it was warranted.

Things had changed. Things had bloody well changed, and it was high time everyone stirred out of the stupor.

Jessica was slightly out of breath when she got in front of the cameras. The swoon was back in full force. She had been in a daze all day, from the moment she heard about this new attack. Possibly she had sensed it coming even before then. But the scene in that house, it had her totally undone. This was it.

"I'm just coming from the house where a ghastly murder has taken place," she told the cameras and mics. "We have reason to believe it was done by the erstwhile serial rapist codenamed Dark Ether. We believe Dark Ether has just committed his first recorded murder. He will now face the full force of the law."

"Detective! Detective," one of the newswomen whom Jessica sort of recognized from TV said. "Yesterday, the outgoing Police Chief of this district at his retirement party claimed a lot of responsibility for the ineffectiveness in apprehending this criminal, is it safe to say that that ineffectiveness is the very reason the situation escalated up to this point."

Jessica realized this for what it was. The newswoman was throwing her a lifeline, asking her to put all the blame of Chief Fenwick, throw him under the boss. News of what transpired at the party last night had probably made rounds, everyone making what they did of that.

What was obvious without doubt was that the Chief had unfairly put the spotlight on them in the way that he did. This was mercy and the chance for revenge being offered her. With one statement, she could have Fenwick's exit from the force a very shameful one like he no doubt thought he had averted with that weepy speech of his.

But Jessica couldn't deny her complicity in whatever charges people leveled at their department. She had after all been one half of the officers directly in charge of the case out in the field. Whatever one was guilty of, all invariably were.

"Please understand that we have been doing all we could in the circumstances," Jessica said, knowing she was about to commit herself in a weird way. "Up till this point, the criminal known as Dark Ether has been very careful. Up till this point.

We believe something must have happened to upset him, enough for this escalation to take place. But whatever it was also got him off balance, and we now have certain clues about the sort of person he is. The case should be concluded soon enough. Thank you."

The newswoman who had asked the question seemed to glare at her as she fired yet another question, "you said earlier that with this murder will now, I quote, 'face the full force of the law.' Might I ask why you say that? Is it because you and your department had been lax, probably because several victims in, you still did not consider the rape of these women a serious crime enough? You didn't think rape warranted the full force of the law?"

Yup, it had happened. Jessica had struck a nerve by rejecting the lifeline that had been offered her and refusing to throw Fenwick under the bus. Now they would hunt her, punish her, forever biting at her heels. Unless she really did close this case.

"I'm sorry," she said to the cameras. "But those are all the questions we will be taking today." She turned around towards the house. But when she looked up, there was James standing there in the doorway, looking at her. Jessica sighed and headed towards the ambulance instead.

"Evidence? What new evidence?" he wondered aloud as he paused the news footage and rewound it to Jessica's statement again. With earphones plugged into his ears, the darkness of the room was especially accentuated by the silence of it all.

The gloom of that all so stuffy room was lit solely by the glare of the PC on which he viewed the footage. If it were lit up a bit more, perhaps one would see the several discarded wraps of potato chips, soda bottles, and a rucksack. On the walls above it all, slightly reflected even now, were pictures.

Enlarged, regular paper printed pictures. They were pictures of several young girls, several of them blonde. Their names were typed out boldly underneath the pictures.
The sound of crinkling paper filled the room as he dug his fingers into a pack of Doritos. He rewound the footage one more time, still trying to figure out what sort of evidence the detective might have been talking about. Or was it a bluff?

It could very well be a triggering bluff. An often-used technique. He rewound the footage yet again, trying to read the lines of her face for any hints, anything which might betray emotions of mischief or misdirection.

He screamed suddenly and paused the video. His heart rate had suddenly spiraled, become erratic. Had he really seen what he thought he had? Clicking on the mouse again, he selected a portion of the footage and played.

Jessica had just finished answering the journalist's questions and was turning away. As she did so, the locks of her raven black hair got caught in a sudden draft of wind and spread about. He paused the video.

"Woah," he said. "Woah."

He slid off his seat and hurried to the walls, moving from picture to picture until he found the one he wanted. The most recent one. The picture of the only non-blonde. Emily Baker.

He ripped the picture off the wall and raced back to the PC. He placed the picture against the screen, side by side with Jessica's face. Oh, fuck. He couldn't believe what he was seeing. Oh, shit. Oh, shit. He skipped the footage forward some minutes.

Meredith Gilliam's picture comes up on screen. Side by side, Meredith and Emily bear remarkable resemblances to each other. His heart was a cannon booming off staccato shots in his chest. He took the footage right backwards and stopped on Jessica.

"Ohhhh, God. This is precious. Precious," he said, chuckling, his mouth suddenly watering.   If the two girls represented anything like a series, then the good detective looked exactly like the next step. This shit was fucking priceless.

Frank threw his gear into the backseat of his car and turned around as Jessica approached him. The ambulance had left with the victim's body and the journalists, having seen the show to the end, had begun to pack up.

He took one look at her, saw how exhausted she was and spread out his arms for her. Jessica walked right into his embrace. "Too much?" he asked. "Too much," she said. "I never thought it would get to this point. It just—I thought—I thought—"

Jessica found herself suddenly bawling against Frank's chest, soaking up his chest as the image of the victim riddled with all those multiple stab wounds flashed through her mind. How did it ever come to this? Frank's strong arms held her, soothed her, smoothening her hair as she cried.

"I'm guessing it didn't go well with the newsmen," he said.
That drew Jessica from her sadness with a flash of annoyance. "Silly
bunch, those," she said, wiping her tears. "They wanted an offering,
someone to roast. I wouldn't give them Fenwick, so I guess it will
have to be me."

"Rough," Frank said, sucking air through his teeth. "And who's this
new arrival?" Jessica turned around just in time to see a 2019 Lincoln
Navigator car roll to a halt. The door slid open, and an African-
American male probably in his early fifties stepped out. He looked
around with an air of authority, spotted Jessica and started marching
towards them.

Jessica recognized them. It was their new Chief. Braxton. Gregory
Braxton. She snapped off a salute as he came to a halt before them.
"Detective Taylor, I suppose," Braxton said.
"Yes, sir," she told him. They shook hands. "And this is my husband,
Frank Taylor. He's a forensic photographer with the department."
"How do you do?" Braxton said, shaking Frank's hand.
"How do you do?" Frank said. "Welcome to the precinct."
"Ah, well. Looks like I've arrived at the most inopportune moment. I
was just getting off the airplane when I heard," Braxton said.
"An ugly incident," Jessica said.

"That didn't have to be," the new Chief said.
Right, Jessica thought. So soon off the plane and already handing out
reprimands.

"I assure you that we've got all hands-on deck, trying to remedy this,
sir," Jessica told him.
"I certainly hope so," the chief said. "I'll be looking to have all your
files on the case as soon as possible."
"Of course, s—"

Jessica's phone broke out suddenly with its ringtone. An awkward
silence descended among the three of them with this rude intrusion.
"Go on, take it," the Chief said.

"Alright, sir," Jessica said, turning around to grab the phone out of her pocket. She felt very embarrassed as she said, "hello."
"Hello, Mrs. Taylor." It was—
"Imelda. What's the problem? Why are you calling?" Jessica said, not even trying to hide her irritation.

"I'm sorry, Mrs. Taylor. But it's the young junior master," Imelda said.
Junior master? Who the fuck was she talking ab—
"Matthew? Why? What's up with him?"
Frank hurried up to her at the mention of his son's name.
"He slumped, Mrs. Taylor."
"What?" Jessica said. Confused. He waved Frank to pause with his worried looks while she got to the root of the matter.
"Slumped. Passed out. The young Mr. Matthew," Imelda told her.
"he was watching TV when suddenly, he fell. I just called the ambulance and I—"
"We're on our way," Jessica said and hung up.

The Name's Matthew "What do you mean by nothing's wrong with him?" Frank asked, staring confusedly at the doctor.
They were seated in an air-conditioned office that was several degrees colder than usual. Kind of like the doctor wanted to freeze his ball off. Jessica tried not to think it had anything to do with the fact that the plaque on the desk said his name was Sven Siegfried.

"What I mean is there is nothing physically wrong with him," the doctor continued. "He isn't exactly suffering from any disease, no hint of food poisoning or anything like that. It's possible he just suffered a dizzy spell or a heat stroke or something like that."
Jessica thought it typical that he would think of heat strokes in these climes.

"Or quite possibly too, it was borne of psychological causes. Otherwise, there's nothing really the matter with him."
Jessica had never seen Frank look as he did in that office. And he was furious still as they walked down the parking lot with Matthew. He had that Bible still with him. Imelda hadn't forgotten to send it along with the ambulance.

"I can't believe this," Frank was saying as he bounded on ahead of them. Jessica brought up the rear with Matthew in the middle. "I thought we were making headway. I really thought we were making headway, young man. But you've decided to mess things up with your attention seeking antics."

"Frank," Jessica said, trying to get him to stop.
"No, let me. Let me, Jess," Frank said. "First, it was him being rude, now this."

He turned to face Matthew. "We were in front of our new boss today. We were talking to the new Chief, under pressure with a case, and then we get called about you. Only to find out you were faking. Do you have any idea what—"

"Okay, enough," Jessica said, butting in. The two curly haired men turned to face her.
She walked up past Matthew, grabbed Frank by the arm and pulled him aside.
"That is no way to talk to your son, Frank. And you should apologize," she said.
"What the hell?" he said, giving her a look that said he thought she was crazy. "Don't you realize how he—"

"Yes, Frank. I was there. But he is a hurting child," she told him. "The world hasn't exactly gone easy on him. To lose one's mother and then find oneself confined to the psych ward not so long afterwards has got to be tough. You think he's trying to get attention? I think so too. But yelling at him isn't the way to get him out of it. So yes, I do think you need to apologize."

Frank looked from her to Matthew, confused. Then realizing he wasn't getting out of this, he walked up to his son.
"Hey, big guy." He sighed and put a hand on Matthew's shoulder. "I shouldn't have yelled back there.

Things are a bit rough and uh... I guess I'm out of touch with um... what I'm trying to say is, I'm sorry. I really shouldn't have yelled. It is my hope that we can both meet each other halfway and come to a

better understanding of each other, okay?"
Matthew gave him a blank faced stare, and finally, after some long
moments, nodded. Frank nodded as well and went back to Jessica.
"That wasn't tough at all," he muttered under his breath.

Jessica chuckled and kissed him on the cheek. "You'll be fine. But go
on. Go shake it off. I'll drive Matthew home. You, go cool off
somewhere. Meet us home with a clear mind."

Frank couldn't help smiling as he kissed her back on the forehead.
"Alright, catch you later."
He snapped off a salute at Matthew before heading off to his car.
Jessica took in a deep breath before turning to the youngster.

She watched him from the rear-view mirror as she drove on the way
home. He had his head resting against the rolled-up window in the
back seat, with that same blank faced expression of his. The Bible
was clutched even still against his chest.
"That's an interesting book you've got there, Matty," Jessica said.
"Can I call you Matty?"

"The name's Matthew," he said matter-of-factly, without even the
slightest hint of malice or otherwise. "And this is a Bible."
"Alright," Jessica said, nodding. "A Bible. And do you take it
everywhere with you?"

Matthew nodded. "The Bible is the Key. The key to freedom and
new life."
"So, what does that make you? A Christian or a Jew?"
"A Christian," Matthew said. "The Jews lost their way with God and
lost their birthright."

"Ouch," Jessica said, staring in the mirror at him. "I've got a couple
of Jewish friends who might not like hearing that."
Matthew continued to stare on at nothing, like what she said had
absolutely nothing to do with anything.

"Your Bible," she said again, realizing she was starting to sound really antagonistic about that book. "Did the doctors and personnel at the hospital give it to you? Was it mandated that you have it?"
"A friend gave it to me," came the reply.
"Oh. At the hospital? This friend of yours is still back there?" she said.
Matthew sighed. What do you know, a human reaction, Jessica thought.

"No," Matthew said. "He died."
"Oh? Oh," Jessica said, looking into the mirror. How much hurt had this kid seen? "I'm—I'm—I'm sorry. I didn't know. I wouldn't have…"

She realized Matthew still had that disinterested look in his eyes. Nothing touched him, she realized. Nothing.
"I'm sorry," she said. And let it go.

She drove on some minutes more in the awkward silence. It felt so oppressive she began to get fidgety. She wanted to pick up her phone and send someone a text, probably catch up with the forensic team on whether they had truly found anything.

She hadn't planned to lie or bluff about shit on camera, but once she had, she really hoped it worked in spooking the Ether into slipping up, or at least turned out to be true. She couldn't really send a text while driving, and a call would warrant discussing the dastardly parts of the case in front of a kid. A stressed kid at that. Jessica decided to put on some music. She was stretching her hand towards the stereo when—

"You're in charge of the Dark Ether case?" Matthew said, finally, catching Jessica off guard.
"Yes," she said, glancing at him on the mirror again. "Why? How did you know that?"
"I saw you on TV," he said.

Right, Jessica thought. Would they have to have a discussion on viewing choices? Jessica hoped it never came to that.
"May I have your phone? I'd like to check something out online," he said.

"Oh, okay. Sure," she said as she clicked it open and handed her phone over backwards to him. She heard his fingers rattling off on the screen as he typed something on the keypad.
"So, you saw me, huh? On TV?" she said. She realized that for the first time, he was looking right at her as he took intermittent glances from the phone to the rear-view mirror.

"I did."
"Imelda said you were watching TV when you passed out. Was it me you were watching at the time?"
"Yes," he told her.
"Okay, then. Would you like to talk about why that happened? Why you passed out?"
"No," he said with a tone of finality as handed the phone over back to her. "Thank you."

"You're welcome, I guess," she said. She didn't have to force anything. This conversation had been much longer than she could anticipate. With time, perhaps, whatever barrier there was remaining between them would crumble too.
Matthew had exited off whatever he had been doing on the phone when she handed to him. But when she checked again later on, she saw he had been looking at girls. Dark Ether's victims.

Nightmares of the Lucid Kind
It was just after midnight when Jessica woke up. She had taken what was meant to be a quick nap just after fixing Frank a dinner snack for when he came back. Sleeping the sleep of the dead like she seemed accustomed to these days, she hadn't even heard the son of a bitch get back.

He currently lay in bed with her, properly undressed and sound asleep. She knew when she asked him later, he would say she looked stressed out and he just didn't want to wake her, kind of like how she didn't want to wake him either right now, still she would have appreciated it if he had. Now she didn't even know if he had eaten. Chances were she wasn't going to go back to sleep for a very long time.

There was her phone to keep her busy, there were the case files she had borrowed home once again, just in case there was something she had missed. She knew there were people who would ask how she still managed to sleep when there were always terrible things going on around her. She sometimes asked that question of herself, but she knew the answer. She was only human. She needed to sleep. Getting so highly strung up with any case could lead to a burn out, and then, she would be very much useless in all instances that required her help.

She checked her phone. There were three missed calls, all from Frank. That had probably been him calling to ask whether to buy dinner on the way home and what she would like. There were two texts from him on WhatsApp querying exactly that. There were other texts from work. The Forensic team still hadn't found anything that could bring them any closer to identifying who the Dark Ether was. There was a text from James. She ignored that one. At this rate, she only trusted what he had to say, when there were other people within earshot.

James hadn't always been like this. It was just… James hadn't always been like this.

Jessica gave a few lazy scrolls through all her social media feeds to see if there was anything new going on. For the most, it was just the usual attempts at humor and sensationalism. It was easy to get sucked right in, but not yet. She had stuff to do, some wrangling to do with work as well. She got off the bed.

Light footed and fast, Jessica had once upon a time been nicknamed the Ghost for how easy it was for her to sneak up on anybody. That was for when she wasn't even trying. She just flitted in and out of spaces and then she was gone. That was quite like right now when she checked the kitchen to find Frank had gotten to his dinner after all and washed up after himself. He had also brought home some pizza which now lay on the kitchen table.

Imelda had been doing the last of her cleaning when Jessica went up
to sleep. Surfaces looked spotless and shiny in the light of the moon
coming through the window. Napkins and washcloths had been hung
up in their proper spaces. The windows were all washed up and shut.
But for Frank's new entry, the trash had been taken out. Sweet
Imelda. She was only ever efficient.

She was about to turn and head back to the bedroom when she
noticed there was light coming out of the laundry room. She didn't
think there was anything odd about that beside oversight and was
going to turn it off when she saw a shadow move inside. Jessica
froze.

Her heart began to punch the insides of her chest. Who was that? As
far as she knew, there were only three humans in this house. They
were, Frank, Matthew, and herself. Frank was pretty much still in the
bedroom where she left him. That meant it was probably Matthew in
the laundry room. But it was way past midnight. Why the fuck was he
up, and what was he doing in the laundry room? But then, there was
also that other likely answer, wasn't there?

Each and every of the Dark Ether's victims—at least those lucky to
have survived him—talked about how he just seemed to sneak up on
them from out of nowhere. Many of them recalled having locked
their doors beforehand, but it didn't matter the type of security, the
Ether seemed to always already be in the house before it all. The cops
knew that wasn't likely.

Dark Ether just always knew his targets beforehand and did his best
to research precisely what would be needed to gain access into their
spaces. At Meredith's house, for instance, they had found the hinges
of her back door amply lubricated. It would have been easy to locate
him through his tools and their likely purchases, if only the Ether
wasn't so keen on improvisation.

The lube he used on the door had been nothing but KY jelly, and
there was no telling how many people owned that shit or had bought
it most recently. That made him once again, a ghost. So, was that him
hiding in her laundry room? And what would her colleagues say he

used in gaining access to her house? Jessica realized that with Dark Ether's recent bloodlust, it was very likely that if that was him in the laundry room, she wouldn't live long enough to find out how he did it.

Jessica tiptoed back to the kitchen. There was the complete set of knives in the rack. She very much wanted to grab one of them, but she also knew there were a high number of bloody domestic accidents that could have been averted if the spooked party had reached for the deadliest weapon in the house.

There were two sets of handyman tools in the house. One set lay out in the garage, waiting for whenever work called upon them. Jessica pulled the fourth drawer beneath her sink for the second set. She grabbed the hammer. A couple of blows to choose parts of the arms and legs would be very well seen for the trained defensive strikes that they were.

One leaden foot after the other, hammer clutched behind her, Jessica tiptoed onwards towards the laundry room. The shadow within the lights was moving. Jessica had been semi-asthmatic as a child, and it chose moments like these to force a comeback at her. The air in front of her seemed all fogged up and dense suddenly, and she was forced to breathe out of her mouth to keep her mind and vision clear. She was getting close now.

The door hadn't been shut all the way through, and there was more than a slice of a crack through which the light within streaked out. All Jessica had to do was get to that slice for her view of whoever kept throwing their shadow on that streak of light. Readying her hammer, she flattened herself on the wall directly opposite the door and began to slide along it. Her heart seemed to have abandoned its home in her chest long ago, and was now beating somewhere closer to her throat, trying to choke her out some more.

Jessica slid on and slid on along the wall, until she came to that slice of light. The simplest explanations with the fewest assumptions. There were practically just three of them in the house. If she had left Frank in the bedroom, it had to be Matthew in the laundry room. Jessica heaved a silent sigh of relief when she saw it really was him.

She was just about to push the door slightly open and crack a joke when he turned slightly, and she saw what he was doing. He was jerking off. What the fuck?! The possibility of that hadn't crossed Jessica's mind in the slightest. Why the hell was he here? He had a bathroom in his room.

What the fuck was wrong with boys and their unending need to explore? That was when she saw precisely what he was doing. He had a piece of fabric in his hand, and he was jerking off to it. He was jerking off to her panties.

Jessica felt her knees go weak and she clasped an arm over her mouth as she slid down the wall.
Calm down! Calm the fuck down, Jessica! He is a teenager. At that fucking age, all boys are such raunchy perverts!

Then his words filtered out to her over his moans and groans. "Yeah, bitch," he said. "Take it. You're a slut. You love my man-seed. You want it, don't you? I know you want it, because you're a slut."
The alarm bells went berserk in Jessica's mind. There was a fire. There was a blaze out here, and that shit had to be put out. But even as she thought that, she was running away from the laundry room. Her palm clasped over her mouth, she was running away. There would be no explaining that shit. There would be no explaining why she was surprising him with a hammer in the dark and shit, all the ways that could go wrong.

Nothing made sense right now, Jessica thought as she slipped back into her bedroom. Nothing made sense and it was because of all these thoughts and notions and emotions swirling through her head space. But if she could just go back to sleep, if she could just go back to sleep. She lifted the pillow, put the hammer underneath it, raised the bed cover and got right in.

That's it, she told herself. The night is dark and terrible. It is a world full of nightmares. The daylight was for making decisions. All would make sense in the daylight.
She found breathing came easier to her now as she thought this. She didn't know how long it was before she fell asleep.

Close Encounters

The waitress set down the tray filled with his order and drifted away.
Frank waved over it all, directing the aroma of his many meal-pieces
as he inhaled. Pure heaven. The Mike & Bee's diner on Euclid
Avenue had been his favorite for many years, and it was here that he
had virtually all of his lunch.

There was a time during their courtship when Jessica accompanied
him on his trips here. Now, those were fun times. But that was then
in the haze of new love when making out time for your partner's
stuff was the order of the day. It was never really expected to last.
It would have been easier if he had been a detective himself. Perhaps,
they would have been partnered up.

Perhaps not, but at least they would be esteemed equally for being in
proximate levels of duty. But not so much. She spent her time all day
with someone who only did as much to hide his disdain for their
marriage. They worked the same cases, took the same rides, had
lunch in the same spots...

Frank ripped his straw free of its wrapping and stuck it inside his cup
of soda. There was nothing like the taste of good old sugar and water
to cool the mind. Usually, he thought as he got ready to wolf down
his meal, there would be lunch from Jessica which he always found a
way to work into the menu of whatever he was having at the diner.
There wasn't any today.

The new case was taking its toll on his wife, apparently. She was
virtually always passed out whenever he got home these days, too far
gone to even notice when he climbed into bed beside her. Then,
there were the new pressures from the media. Frank had read the
online article a few hours ago. He thought the author was a bitch,
plain and simple. If there was any way of remedying that he would.
Even if it meant paying the author a visit himself, but nah. Some
things just didn't work.

There was, of course, Matthew. She acted like she was fine, but Jessica would have to be inhuman, extraterrestrial, a freaking demon to say his presence in the house wasn't affecting her in the slightest.

At least not in these stages of early adjustments.
All he expected nonetheless, was for her to simply try. That was the surest way to make anything work in the first place. That was precisely what made humans so freaking special. They were the only ones who tried.

The tiny bells clinked as the door to the diner swung open. When it slid shut, there was a wild looking man standing in the doorway. He made his way to the counter and leaned on it, one amongst the many placing their orders. Frank saw that the man was surreptitiously making a sweep of the room out the corner of his eyes.

There were a few reasons why Frank picked him out from among the crowd. First, he had a habit of sitting within a clear view of the door. It didn't matter the nature of the place or precisely where he was located, but he had trained himself to always have his eyes on the door.

Usually, he was forever placed so he spotted whoever came in first, giving him ample time to react. When he first told Jessica about it, she had laughed it off, making a joke about him thinking he was a character in a movie about the mob.

Then, there was the fact of the man's general appearance. Perhaps, if Frank was of a more literary bent, he would have said the man looked something of a rat. He was dressed in haggard worn clothes that had obviously been thrown together without much thought, and probably hadn't been washed in a long time.

He didn't look like he had had a bath in ages, either. At least, he hadn't shaved. His face looked like it was perpetually hiding in the shadows because of the untrimmed beard growing every other way. The pallor of his skin suggested as much too. This guy very rarely came out in the sun.

But it wasn't all this that highlighted him as an interesting fellow. Frank had seen all manner of people come in here, many of them haggard and sickly, but he had never seen this guy. Virtually everyone in the diner was a regular, and that didn't mean they spent their every cent and second here.

This guy was just the first stranger Frank had seen here in a long time, and that spelled trouble. And all that was before he even began his shifty sweep of the place. Frank stretched his feet out some more under the table and slid down, so he was slightly lower in his seat. The man's eyes roved around all the same, and odd as it was, rested on Frank.

They looked at each other for one long moment, then the man straightened up, shifted back from the counter, and started coming towards Frank.

Okay, Frank thought. We are in Troubleville. He regretted not having ordered coffee. He was virtually bereft of weapons. There was nothing heavy enough on his table to serve as such. Whatever there was would be more annoyance than actual deterrent, but he was certain it would do, if he was fast enough. It was only a matter of sliding out the side of his table and letting the weight of his body finishing the rest of the job when he launched it forward.

The man walked all the way up to Frank's table and stopped. Frank looked up at him and glared.
"How may I help you?" he said.
"Mr. Frank Taylor," the man said.
Frank felt his insides twist and go stiff all at the same time. Who was this guy?

"Are you a shepherd or a wolf?" the man said.
"What?" Frank said, confused. His mind was reeling with possibilities of identifying this man.
"Are you a shepherd or a wolf?"
"What the hell are you talking about?"
"Tiffany Bentham."

"What?" Frank said. But the man wasn't done.
"Vanessa Ditko. Brenda Speck. Linsey Corey-Jones. Allysa Martin. Bella Watford. Kaitlyn Malone. Libbie Velasquez. Diane Kint. Emily Baker. Meredith Gilliam. Are you a shepherd or a wolf?"

"I really do not appreciate the tone of—"
The man took a couple of steps back from Frank, then he turned and crashed right into a man with a tray of food. The two of them staggered for a bit as the contents of the man's meal spilled onto the floor. Then Frank's mystery guest righted himself and fled out of the diner.

Frank just sat there flummoxed.

A Kitchen Sink Issue
"What?" Jessica said, incredulously. "And what did he say afterwards?"

"Nothing. The guy just turned and fled. He even bumped into—I don't know, all of it was just funny, if it wasn't also scary," Frank said.

"Shit," Jessica said, pacing about the room. They were in the kitchen and Frank currently had pasta boiling in a pan. "And you say you've never met him?"

"Never," Frank said, almost amusedly. "The entire thing was like a scene out of the twilight zone. I'm sorry. I didn't mean to get you all worked up."

"Get me all worked up?" Jessica said, teetering on the very edge of anger. "It's my job we're talking about here. My investigation. People are getting murdered, for fuck's sakes.

In their own homes, by a motherfucker creeping about in the dark. How can I not be worked up? Every time something related to Dark Ether pops up, I have to be notified, that very minute."
"Okay, okay. I get it," Frank said, walking over to hold her. "I screwed up."

Jessica shrugged him off and continued pacing around the kitchen. "I'm sorry," Frank told her. "I really should have done something or alerted you. I was shocked and confused, that's no excuse. I'm sorry." Jessica heaved a huge sigh and sat down on one of the kitchen stools.

"Come on, describe him to me. What did he look like?" she said. Lifting the pan off the cooker and pouring the spaghetti into a sieve at the sink, Frank did his best to describe the man as perfectly as possible while she listened.

"Hold on a minute," Jessica said. She was sitting still at her seat, her hands held out in front of her like she was trying to focus on something. "Did he have a pink-ish scar over one eye? Might have been a birthmark?"

Frank paused. "Oh, wow. Now that I think about it, he did. I thought it was dirt or some skin disease of some sort."
He turned to face her. "You know that guy?"
Jessica let out a deflated hiss and rested her head on the table. When she raised her head again, her face was free of all the worry creases. She was calmer again.

"Fred Bolton," she said. "It's hard not to miss that guy. He always was a creep. I should have known it was him."
"Really? How do you know him?" Frank said as he poured some sliced onions into the screaming oil.

"He was a cop."
"A cop?" Frank said, turning to face her, gape eyed.
"Yes. Frank and I helped out with one of the cases at his precinct, and he developed something of a crush."
"It'd be hard to see why not. But eish…" Frank turned to continue his cooking.

"It was a professional crush. The guy wanted to be a detective," Jessica said.

"Okay?"

"He said he wanted to be a detective. But he was one of the guys with the least aptitude for it, and James told him so in not so kind words."

"Uhuh."

"This was at the start of the first Dark Ether cases," Jessica continued. "Fred didn't take the incident with James very well. He made us a promise. A bet, if you will. He would be the one to unmask Dark Ether. And then we would be forced to eat our words in shame."

"Right," Frank said with a sigh. "So, what's up with him? Why did he look a mess like he did?"

"Last I heard, he was let off the force. One weird reason or the other. Like I said, the man was a creep. I saw him one time while I was out grocery shopping, and ducked. He had seen me all the same, and came up to me to say so. He looked like he hadn't taken a shower for almost a decade, which is impossible. I apologized for any misgivings and fled. That's it."

"Hmm," Frank said. His back was solid as a rock as he stood there, processing, stirring the sauce in a pan. "An odd tale for an odd man. Do you think he's aware we're married?"

"I don't know. Why?" Jessica said.

"That might explain why he came to me. A proxy for you. It's obvious, whatever the case, he isn't done with you yet."

"It's possible," she said, mulling over it. "I don't know. I didn't consider it."

"Mmhmm," he said.

Jessica realized he was doing that thing again, shutting her out so he could turn the matter this way and that in his mind.

Matthew walked into the kitchen right then.

Between the patter of his feet as he headed to the fridge and the burble of boiling tomato sauce, there was no other sound in the kitchen. Without a word to either his father or Jessica, he opened the fridge, picked out an apple, and began to munch it right there. Jessica watched the two men. With their stiff backs and curly hair, they looked like different versions of the same person. She hadn't considered before, but Jessica just now realized that parents could very well be judged in the light of their children. How had she never thought to do that with Frank?

Was it because there was no chance of her ever giving him any children and she was averse to the option of adoption that she had never considered so crucial an issue? Lord knew the two men already shared more than their physical appearances.

They both had that characteristically oppressive silence with which the shut out the world so tyrannically, leaving them alone in the bubble of their confidence. That was a very powerful point of convergence. So, how much more similar were they?
Take my man seed, you slut. You know you want it because you're a slut.

She hadn't yet told Frank what transpired the other night. She hadn't forgotten his reaction the other day at the hospital when he thought Matthew was just seeking attention. Yet Jessica thought it probably said something ugly that he had raised someone like that.

It was widely held that all fathers were invariably absentee dads, yet it couldn't be denied that for how very little time the hung around, they did in fact influence the upbringing of their children.
Matthew had spent a good percentage of his life in an asylum for kids. But before he went there, what had he seen? What bits of Frank affected him so? Why did he have to go to the asylum in the first place?
Jessica thought it crazy that she had never thought to ask that question, and that Frank had never brought it up either. What the fuck kind of marriage was this? Jessica wondered all of a sudden. Did she and her husband even know each other?
"So, I might be making a trip to Georgia," Frank said out of the blues.

"What?" Jessica said.

He turned to face her.

"There's this conference on forensic science I've been invited to speak on. A small thing really. I didn't think it would pan out. I've been putting off mentioning it, but I just got alerted today that everything is a go, and my presence is very needed."

"This is not cool," Jessica said. "What conference? We're supposed to discuss these things together."

"I know. It's just—You know what? I'll forward you the emails. See what you make of it. It took me by surprise as well. I'm sorry about not mentioning it."

"This is not cool, Frank. Not cool." She sighed. "When's the conference?"

"Saturday, but I'm expected to come in Thursday."

"Wow. Just wow, Frank," she said, crossing her arms.

"I'm sorry, I'm sorry." He rushed over and kissed her on the forehead. "I'll forward you the emails, okay?"

Jessica sighed.

Frank moved away from her, raced to the cooker, and turned around with two piping hot dishes of spaghetti. Jessica saw that Matthew had turned around sometime while they spoke, and he was now watching his father.

"Here you go, lady and gent," Frank said, smiling at them both as he set the dishes on the table. "Dinner is served."

Babylon the Great

Jessica stared at her panty drawer. It didn't look disturbed in the slightest bit, but she was disturbed. She really should have said something the day after she saw Matthew, but she hadn't. Now it was far long gone and without any real evidence, it might seem like a false accusation and begin to breed new forms of resentment between Frank and her.

Yet she couldn't allow it go on any longer. There was nothing right or appropriate about what had happened, and she couldn't stand having to check her undies every time for traces of Matthew's spunk. His man seed. This shit had to stop.

Frank was having a shower. For the fact that she really couldn't bring herself to tell him anything without real solid evidence, she felt it was only apt that he not know. Besides, waiting till she had evidence could only raise questions of why she hadn't spoken up in the first instance. The question of who truly was the weird, possible predator might not be as easy then. If she could put an end to the issue as coolly and quietly as possible, that would be most perfect.

She made her way to the living room. Matthew was seated in front of the TV, watching a sit-com with a laugh track. But he never cracked so much as a smile regardless of what was said or laughed at. Jessica took a seat on one of the couches, pretended to watch TV for a few seconds, then turned to face him.

"Hello, Matthew," she said. "Could I talk to you about something for a moment?"
The boy did not so much as flinch, but kept his gaze fixed on the TV.
He picked the remote nonchalantly and aimed it at the TV.
"It's about what happened the other night. You in the laundry room."

Matthew froze in the very act of changing the TV channel. Jessica saw him spy her out the corner of his eye with a quick glance. Got you there, motherfucker, she thought. So, you're in there after all.

Jessica couldn't decide which angered her more, that he had had the presence of mind to be rude and deceive her all along, or that she had very nearly fallen for his feigned disaffectedness.

"I just wanted to tell you that while I understand your need as a young man to explore your blooming sexuality, I do not appreciate how you went about it."

Matthew let his hand drop with the remote, his eyes stealing intermittent glances at her.

Oh no, you don't, Jessica thought. His silence of noncommittal wasn't going to work this time around. She had spoken to him, and she demanded an answer.

"Do you understand what I just said?" she asked, putting some steel in her voice.

Matthew rose out of his seat slowly, looking so suddenly agitated as he muttered to himself.

"Excuse me? What was that?" Jessica asked, standing up too.

"Babylon the Great, Whore and Mother of many lies."

"What?"

"Babylon the Great, Whore and Mother of many lies," he continued muttering as he walked away from the living room. "Babylon the Great, Whore and Mother of many lies. Babylon the Great, Whore and Mother of many lies. Babylon the Great, Whore and Mother of many lies."

"What? How dare you?" Jessica followed after him.

He had his hands to his temple, shaking his head furiously as he muttered those words on and on.

"You may think you have me fooled with your antics, but not anymore. For as long as you live under this roof, you will be respectful and refrain from inappropriate behavior."

"Liar! Liar! Liar! Liar!" he was screaming now. He took a detour through the hallways and found his way to the kitchen. Jessica followed still.

"Look at me. Look at this house. There is a family here waiting to have you if you would quit fucking things up," she said.
"She uses swear words. Fucking cunt, whore."

The slap lashed out quick before Jessica could stop it. It struck Matthew full on the face and knocked him quiet. He gaped at her, horror red on his face. Then he screamed.
"Aaaaaaarrrrrrrrrrgggghhhh!"

He lunged at her and knocked her down with the full force of his weight. "I'll kill you, you stupid bitch. Whore! Slut! Cunt of Babylon!"
"Matthew! Matthew, stop please. I'm sorry," Jessica said as she tried to fight off the hands reaching for her throat.

"I'll kill you! Stupid bitch! Look in the mirror bitch! Look in the mirror, see who's being hunted! The father knows! The father sees your guilt. See who's being hunted!"

His hands were at her throat now, squeezing, choking, strangling.
"Stop, Matthew! You're hurting me!" Jessica was struggling to focus. All those lessons—all those defensive lessons on what to do when in positions like this, it was all gone. She needed to breathe. She needed him off her. "You're hurting—"
"Stupid whore of—"
"Hey, Matthew!" Frank said, appearing all of a sudden. He hooked his hands into Matthew's underarms and hauled him away. "Get off her!"

Matthew staggered a few feet backwards as he looked at his father and Jessica crawling away from under his feet. Blinded by rage, he hurled himself at them one more time and—
Bam! Frank sent a solid fist to the side of his jaw. It knocked him out cold.

Jessica was standing by the lawn, massaging her neck while the ambulance from the asylum wheeled Matthew out of the house. He was strapped down to the bed, leaving just his head free, and he was screaming and laughing as he went.

"Listen to me, Babylon the Great! He's coming! The Father cometh. He cometh, and he will pass judgment for all your lies! Look into the mirror and see. See who is being hunted! The Father cometh! Babylon the Great, Whore and—"

The ambulance door slammed shut on him, cutting off his words. Jessica couldn't believe it. How had that been in her house? There was no headway with him, the hospital hadn't sent him home better in the slightest. With sentiments like that, there was no telling what he might have done to her were they ever to be alone in the house. Fuck.

Frank was standing beside the ambulance, talking to the hospital personnel. She saw him hand over something that looked exactly like Matthew's Bible. Good. She was glad to be rid of everything that was even remotely of him. The attendants gave Frank a pad, and he scribbled something elaborate on it. When he handed the pad back, Jessica knew that everything was done. Frank shifted backwards as the men got into the ambulance. It roared to life a few moments later, then it was off, rolling away.

Frank started coming towards her, throwing glances now and again at the car rolling down the street. He looked so innocent in his shorts and white tees, and yet—
"Hold it right there," Jessica said.
Frank paused, confused. "Now what?"
"Did you know he was like that? What the hell was that even to begin with?" she said.

"What do you expect me to say? He came from the asylum. I assume they wouldn't let him out if they didn't think he was okay."
"Okay?" she said, incredulously. "He attacked me. I could very well have been killed."

"That's a bit of an overstatement—"
"Overstatement?"
"Okay. That wasn't right. I apologize. I'm sorry."
"Not this time, Frank," she said. She shut her eyes, took in a deep breath, and said, "I don't feel safe sleeping in the same house with you tonight."
"What do you mean by—"

Jessica took several steps backwards from his advance. "You had a trip planned," she continued. "you will go inside, take as many clothes as you need, and leave tonight. Go to some hotel or motel, anywhere, until you have to travel. By the time your trip's over, if everything has cooled, perhaps we'll talk."
"Jessica, this isn't—"
"Just go," she said.
Frank sighed. He turned and walked right into the house. He was gone within an hour.

End of the Line

At about the time Frank's flight left for Georgia, he was seated outside a café in Lakewood, Ohio, with a magazine sprawled in his lap. He had been traipsing along that region for a couple of days now, hoping to catch a glimpse of the man known as Fred Bolton.

He had a feeling the man was on to something which Jessica and her partner had missed, probably on account of arrogance. For some reason, he had felt Jessica's husband was the best person to relate it to, and Frank was looking to give him a chance.

He hadn't planned on spending all that long on the job. Three days were all he had given himself. How hard could it have been? A man like Fred was supposed to be very easy to spot. Yet, having been at it for four days, Frank was almost glad for the extra days afforded him by Jessica kicking him out.

He had had to be very careful with the questions he asked, so Fred wouldn't get forewarned about someone looking for him. He had had to do it without being seen to do it, and while many did indeed know the person he was after, few of them knew precisely where to find him.

He had been spotted at this or that place a couple of days ago. He had stopped over at that joint just yesterday. Whatever the case, it seemed Mr. Bolton was really quite practiced in the art of living off the grid.

Frank took a sip of his coffee. It was a particularly rich brew. He had been discovering some amazing places out here on his mini adventure. Frank acknowledged once again, like all the many explorers before him, that life offered so many opportunities which were often blotted out from view by the lethargy and monotony of regular life.

It was amazing how much of an insight one could gain into one's life with just a little shift in perspective. For instance, within the pages of the magazine in his lap, Frank had discovered an article dedicated to the Dark Ether investigation.

Freed from the strictures of being so tightly tied to the case, and with questions succinctly posed, Frank appreciated for the first time, how much the investigation was being bungled by ineptitude. His mind had gone back to the other article featuring Jessica, and then— There he was. Frank grabbed his magazine and raised it to his face as slowly and calmly as possible.

Up ahead across the street and trying so desperately to mingle in with the crowd at a newsstand was Fred. He was doing that thing again where he tried not to be obvious as he followed someone with his eyes. But who?

Frank traced an imaginary line of sight from Fred and—Bingo!—it was a young lady with an amazingly full head of luscious black hair.

"Detective Taylor," Chief Braxton said. "It has come to my knowledge that things aren't particularly well at home."
Jessica angled her head sharply at him as if to ask, 'how so?'
"I'm hoping this is not in any way hampering your efficiency in handling the Dark Ether case?" the Chief finished.

"Chief Braxton, we all have our private lives, and I believe we all have our private struggles. But the hallmark of professionalism has always been our ability to separate personal lives from work and I'm yet to hear anyone complain about me not being professional."
Chief Braxton smiled. "But yours is a peculiar case, isn't it?

You're married to a member of the force here and I believe he's on the same case as you. How do you intend to keep both spheres of your life distinct, when they are so tightly intertwined?"
"May I please ask where this is coming from?" Jessica said. She was feeling very pissed suddenly.

"A couple of us sat down, and we decided it was a little weird that throughout this case, you and your team haven't turned up a single lead or evidence that might lead to the apprehension of this criminal."

"We are just as stumped, sir. We've got—"
"Your job is not to get stumped, detective. Your job is to produce results."
Jessica was glad that the Chief had drawn the blinds before this chat began, but she felt his voice that time was loud enough to render that redundant.

"Yes, that's true," she said. "But we're also dealing with someone who is very good, precise and knows just how to cover his tracks."
"And what's your angle on that?" Chief Braxton asked. "Where does that lead you? If he's that good at covering his tracks, probably because he knows what we look out for, is it possible that he's an officer?"

"Not necessarily. These days, anyone with an internet connection, which is everyone, can learn about our methods."
"But it's possible, isn't it?" Chief Braxton leaned closer with his elbows on the desk, fingers of both hands together. "I've read Chief Fenwick's report on you. It was full of the highest praise and flattering remarks. He held you in high esteem. I'm yet to see anything which would warrant such sentiments.

Word around is Fenwick was grooming you to be his successor. But it also seems to me like he surrounded himself with the ineptest of officers. I don't want to end up like him, telling sob stories at my retirement to garner sympathy. I want to walk out with my head held high. I can only do that with a department which works. You've got two weeks. Two weeks, detective, to come up with something worthwhile in this case, or I'm having it transferred. Is that clear?"
"Yes, sir."
"Dismissed."

As Jessica left the Chief's office, she realized what that had been about. She was being warned. The Chief was cleaning house soon, ridding himself of Fenwick's loyalists. The only way to survive that was to beat this absurd ultimatum and prove you were worth something after all.

Eyes followed her each way she turned as she walked through the stationhouse. Sympathetic eyes, eyes joyful of her descent and hoping to replace her. She was already at his door before Jessica realized where her feet had led her.
She rapped her knuckles on the door and James's head shot up from behind his PC.
"Basement/photocopier, now."
She was off on her way before he could respond.

Frank chuckled to himself as he followed Fred through the streets. Pin a tail on the tail. He wondered what movie archetype Jessica would accuse him of playing now.

He kept a safe distance from his quarry, tried not to look conspicuous while at it. Emily Baker. Meredith Gilliam. They had both had black hair.

Who was this girl Fred was tailing? Frank wondered whether to call in to the stationhouse now, put an end to all this. But perhaps, it would be a little too premature. Just a little more time to ensure it was all concrete, that's all that was needed.

The girl made a turn down a row of apartment buildings. Fred stood for a while to scan his surroundings. Frank pretended to check out a poster on the wall. A few moments later, Fred made the turn. Frank followed as quickly as possible.

He made the turn and found it led to an alley, but no one was in sight. He hurried down along, hoping to catch sight of either Fred or the girl. Suddenly, he found himself next to a window with the blinds only halfway shut. Beyond the blinds, he saw her. The girl. She was standing in the middle of a room and taking her blouse off. Was he in there? Was Fred in there?

Frank drew a little closer to the window, wondering what else he could see. He did not hear the man coming behind him. The move was fast and suddenly there was something papery pressing against his face.

Frank jumped to shake his attacker off and just at the same time, realized there was also something powdery about the sheet being pushed right in his nostrils. He recognized the smell and immediately felt his brain go cold as ice. Dark Ether. It was Dark—
Frank saw the floor rush up at him all of a sudden, and darkness claimed him.

The door to the copying room slid open and Jessica turned as James made his way in. His face was a leaden mask, hard and unreadable. Jessica felt a pang of guilt hit her.

"There's trouble, James. We've got trouble," she said. "Chief Braxton wants to clean house, and he's gunning for us."
"Yeah? I heard," James said, with a noncommittal shrug.
"We've got to do something, otherwise he'll—"
"Why should I care? This case hasn't exactly been—"
Jessica threw herself at him and kissed him full on the mouth. He held her close to him as they kissed for a few passionate seconds, then he pushed her aside.

"You," he said with all the bitterness in the world on his face.
"You've ignored me all these months, played me for a—"
"I had a child over, James. I had to play the perfect wife and mother," she told him.

"Yeah? And how did that work out for you?" he said.
She kissed him again, opening her mouth to let the sweet invasion of his tongue.

"I've missed you. How I've missed you, James," she said when they broke. "You've got it? Tell me you've got it, please."
"I'm never without it," James said, raising a clear plastic bag of dark reddish powder.

The smell hit Jessica again and she smiled as the swoon returned. Dark Ether. It had been a while. She was unzipping the fly of her pants as she rushed over to get some.

Dark Father

When Frank came to, he found himself in the gloom of a darkened room. Everywhere around him was a thick fog he couldn't yet penetrate, and in the air was the stench of something ripe. Frank realized he was all bound up to a chair and opened his mouth to scream for help.

"I wouldn't scream, if I were you," someone said in the dark. "It wouldn't be wise to draw any attention here considering everything I know."

"Wh—who are you? What do you want?" Frank said. The tremble in his voice was something odd, uncharacteristic, and yet, there it was.
A click, and the light came on in the room. It came from a tiny lampstand on a table in the corner of the room, and Fred was seated beside it.

"Mr. Taylor," he said as he leaned forward out of the shadows. "How are you feeling?"
"Exactly like you wanted me to. You drugged me you son of a bitch," Frank said.

"I'm sorry. But it was the only way to get you here," Fred said. "When I heard there was someone asking around after me, I knew it was you. Contacting you in public like I did was a huge risk, but it was the safest choice for all involved. And it paid off in the end, didn't it, Mr. Dark Ether?"
"Stop calling me that," Frank said.

On God, the guy was obsessed. In the poor lighting they had, Frank hadn't noticed at first, but taped to the walls were pictures of every of Dark Ether's victims. He couldn't believe it, but this was almost apt dwelling for this rat faced fucker.

"Tiffany Bentham," Fred said, rising from his seat.
"What?"
"Vanessa Ditko." He was taking steps, getting closer, with each name
that he called.

"Oh, God, not this again," Frank said.
"Brenda Speck. Linsey Corey-Jones. Allysa Martin. Bella Watford.
Kaitlyn Malone. Libbie Velasquez. Diane Kint. Emily Baker.
Meredith Gilliam. Are you a shepherd or a wolf?"

"I don't know what the hell that's supposed to mean, but I get that
you think I'm the Dark Ether. You couldn't be more wrong, my
friend. I am not who you think I am."

"Oh, yeah?" Fred said. "So why haven't you screamed then? You're
not gagged. You're supposed to be frightened of me, I mean, I'm
supposed to be dangerous, but you haven't uttered one cry for help.
Why is that?"

Frank opened his mouth to say something, paused, and shut it again.
He didn't have anything to say to that.
"You had us all fooled, Mr. Taylor," Fred said, speaking slowly like
someone giving a most important lecture. "You had everyone
stumped. No evidence. None whatsoever. I wonder, is it because
knowing police procedure, you're very thorough going in, or if you
clean up after yourself when you eventually do visit the crime scene
Mr. Forensic Photographer? I think it's a mixture of both."

Frank's hands had begun to hurt, sitting as he was. He glanced at his
bounds—rope wrapped around him—checking for weaknesses. He
shifted slightly and shrunk inwards into himself. That freed him up
some.

"You know, the big question was why," Fred kept on talking. "Why
was the Dark Ether doing what he was doing? All those poor girls? I
followed the investigation closely.

All he ever did was break in and rape them. But he'd do it so methodically, without any of the maniacal explosions, that showed he knew precisely what he was doing. But why?

Did he have a thing against blondes? That was the only bit as far as psychological leanings went. Without a proper frame of reference, the question couldn't be answered.

"They laughed at me; you know?" Fred said, stroking his chin as he recalled. "Detective Reeves and Detective Taylor. Your wife. She laughed at me when I said I just might prove my worth by finding out just who the Dark Ether was. So, imagine my surprise when I finally found out the frame of reference and it was her."

Fred's voice was exciting now as he continued, "we couldn't have figured it out going about it the way we were. The girls all similar looking and of the same build pointed to someone in particular, but whom? Who was it that had inspired such dastardly acts? Usually, it's the perp's mother or someone as close, but how could we identify this someone in a city so vast?

None of the psych-profiles we put out into the public brought anything of worth. Then one day, Detective Taylor is on the screen, and boom! There it was. Two girls—two girls representing a seismic shift in the case. Two girls, black of hair, one of them murdered. Who could inspire such, but Detective Taylor?

As she stood there on TV, I saw in her, the model for the two girls who had most recently been attacked. But she had been in the public eye all along, since the beginning of the case.

"What had she done that would cause him to attack her all so suddenly? I couldn't find anything. If it hadn't been done publicly, then perhaps it was done privately. And which was only fitting seeing as monsters are usually bred behind closed doors.

So, I looked. I looked. Who could she have hurt enough in private that could be lashing out so violently? She wasn't anybody's mother. But she was someone's wife. Yours.

"So, I dug into you. Like I said, all we ever really needed was that frame of reference because I didn't have to dig so far. The good Detective wasn't your first wife. Matter of fact, it was a certain Lillian Taylor. And guess what, Lillian was blonde.

As I moved through pictures of her, I saw that she would have fit into the lineup of the nine other girls, if she wasn't slightly older and their model. What were the girls?

Outlets for venting your frustrations, or were they a cover up, misdirection from another crime? It didn't surprise me to find out that your wife was dead. Not one bit. Ruled an accident, but I had my suspicions. And turns out I wasn't alone. Matthew Taylor, teenaged and locked in an asylum, believed his mother had been killed, courtesy, judgment of the father. And you fit the profile.

"You alone in this city have been married to two women who could serve as the prototypes of the girls who had been attacked. You alone of all possible suspects work closely enough with the case to ensure there are no material evidence to let suspicion fall on you. You alone are possibly the Dark Ether."

"Wow," Frank said, his voice level as ever. "Seems like such a small basis to hinge an enormous investigation. Thin ice, my friend."
"It's you," Fred said, rushing towards Frank and dropping to his knees. He spoke with such pleading and earnestness as if to convince Frank that his words were true.

"It's you, Mr. Taylor. I know it's you. I know it as much as I know the sun shines. I know it with my own beating heart. I knew it the moment I saw you that day, back at the diner. You have suffered, just like me.

You know what it means to be mocked and humiliated, just like me. But you have risen above it all, risen to glorious heights.
"What are you, shepherd or wolf?

Are you going to guide other lost sheep like me into the path of glory and reclamation, or are you going to let your marvelous work be wiped out? It's you, Mr. Taylor. I know it's you. Show me the way. Show us the way."

Fred was weeping now, weeping on his knees, rocking back and forth while he held Frank's bound hand, kissing it. "It's you. It's you. I know it's you."

Frank looked down on him with all the contempt in his eyes. Pathetic. He could now get why people like this inspired only feelings of revulsion and the meanest treatment. If you behaved like a dog, you could only be treated like a dog. Unless you somehow found the courage to rise.

"Unbind me," Frank said.
Fred whipped his head up at the power and authority in that voice. He moved quickly to the command and made short work of it. Frank's joints creaked and cracked as he rose out of his seat. He turned this way and that to loosen himself some more. He glanced around at the posters on the wall, they and the other inscriptions. The Father. Dark Ether. Dark Father. Please, show me the way. "Well, well, well," he said. "You've been very busy. Now, let's get you started properly."

...Shall Make You Free...

With enough time and patience, you could figure out the routines of any organization or institutions. When it went to work, when it took its breaks, and when it ceased operation for the night. Matthew had had his figured out a long time ago, but he had never had cause to put this knowledge to use. Now was the time.

Babylon the Great. She had tried to mother him, but she had been deemed unworthy. He saw it in his every look, heard it in every inflection of his voice. The Father was displeased, and so she would pay. She tried to trick him, tried to guilt him into taking responsibility for her sins. But why did she keep such unchaste items around the house if not to cause him to sin? Such was the greater sin. God who saw all, knew all, and judgment was coming.

Judgment was coming and the Father would bring it. Her cup was full and running over. The time had come for her to be cast aside, and so she would. The Father had said as much. He heard it in the secret things of his voice. Perhaps, that was why the Father had struck him.

Her judgment was his and his alone to deliver. He had tried to bring it too quickly before the appointed time and the Father was displeased and he had been cast into the outer darkness. But he would show his loyalty. To the Father, he would prove his worth. Perhaps then the Father wouldn't cast him out so much. Perhaps then he would stay.

Matthew heard the click of a latch seven rooms away. The latch. The final call for the night. That was the sound of the orderly making his final patrol of the night. After which, sleep would come. Matthew counted heartbeats.

There were nine hundred and seventy-two heart beats within which the regular human settled fully into the realms of sleep. If he was going to be successful, Matthew needed the orderly to be totally lost to the world before he made a move. And so he counted.

It was many years ago when Matthew first felt the Father's displeasure. At the time, the Father had been just Frank Taylor. Up on TV came the news of a girl who had been raped and very near strangled to death.

They had called her a young girl, but they had lied, because when Matthew looked up, though her face had been blurred on screen, he saw she was Lillian.

She was Lillian, and so he screamed.
At the time, Lillian Taylor was the woman who had also been known as mother. She rushed into the living room and picked him up and asked him what was wrong.

He told her Lillian was on TV, Lillian had been hurt, but TV Lillian also had a different name. It was Tiffany Bentham. And so Lillian did not know that Tiffany was also Lillian. But she was Lillian and Matthew knew it.

This was also the time when Matthew knew that Lillian-Mother had another smell. A smell he did not like. He knew that not only he knew it, because whenever she had that smell on her, Frank Taylor's face stiffened. Matthew saw that the shape and structure of his muscles shifted and that was because the smell also displeased him.

The only other time Matthew saw that shift was when another hurt Lillian came on TV. Matthew knew then that the Father was judging. Five hundred and thirty-seven.

Lillian died. They said it was an accident. But Matthew knew different. The Father had judged. He announced it to all he came around, proudly. The Father had judged. The Father had gotten rid of that stench once and for all time. And though nobody understood what he meant, it seemed his proclamation displeased Father. That was the first time he was cast into outer darkness.

It was here in the regions beyond that he first came to know what that stench was. Sex. He smelled it on everybody. The doctors, the nurses, his woman-fellow inmates after certain visits from the orderlies. Sex. It permeated everything with its foul odor. Matthew knew then why Father had hated it so much.

Nine hundred and seventy-four. Matthew caught himself as he nodded off to sleep. It was time.

He grabbed his Bible. The Sword of Truth. The Bible held the key. Matthew turned it sideways and stared. To the untrained eye and impatient mind, the Bible looked neat and unaltered. But the spine had been altered alright.

A stable hand, a steady heartbeat and a patient mind had fixed it back. Matthew ripped the black binding off the spine, revealing a set of keys that had been glued right on. Keys he had pilfered one way or the other with speed and precision.

An insertion in the keyhole and a slow twist had the door open before him. Matthew walked into the hallway. He didn't have anything to fear of security guards. At 03:15am, he knew they were all sound asleep. There was another door ahead up fifty yards away. Matthew fished out the key, without breaking stride.

Jessica was Babylon the Great, just like the rest of them. The stench was on her too, no matter how faint, but that was alright. The Father would deliver judgment, and he would be there to witness it.

Hi James, Bye James

There was music booming in the house when Frank knocked. He didn't know if the quaking he felt in his chest was truly his or if it came from the speakers. He took a fearful glance around at the street, then knocked again.

"Coming!" he heard James say. Moments later, the door clicked open, and they were face to face.
James looked confused for a moment before going, "Hey, Frank. What are you doing here? Why do you look that way?"
Frank cast another fearful look down the street and pushed past James into the house.

"I need a drink."
James staggered aside. He stuck his head out for a second to scan the street, then he shut the door.
"Hey, Frank, what's going on? Jessi said you were out of town. Why are you dressed that way?"

"I didn't travel. I didn't go anywhere. I was undercover," Frank said. His voice was all jittery and quaky and tremulous.
"Undercover?" James said, taking another look at him. In contrast to his bare-chested host, Frank was dressed in an overcoat that was several sizes too big and topped with a fedora. Jessica would have said he was a character in a Humphrey Bogart movie.

"Yes, undercover. Dark Ether. He—fuck, for chrissakes, a drink, dammit!" Frank snapped.
"Hold on a minute."
James left Frank pacing up and down the living room.

Jessica was doing justice to the last of her meal in the dining room. She had the table all laid out and the room was lit only by candlelight. There was something to being alone and free that often found expression in taste.

She knew eventually, the buzz would die out and then would come lethargy, as every pleasure in life sooner or later dwindled to monotony if indulged long enough. Usually, the contrast was met with frustration, after which came acceptance. Most people never lasted long till the period of acceptance before jumping into some other mode of comfort or distraction.

Jessica knew this, but had not yet decided which way she would tilt when the time finally came.

Nothing new had come up in the Dark Ether case. Not even after several hours of staring at the case file and willing fresh insight to come to her. She was calmer right now solely on account of what had gone down in the basement at the stationhouse earlier on.

Riding on that high, she had decided that perhaps it wasn't so bad if Chief Braxton brought the axe down on her. Sure, it might entail a bit of humiliation, but that was about it. He couldn't exactly fire her, she hadn't done anything wrong. But getting transferred off a case that probably wouldn't be closed in the next decade was pretty much okay.

To the rest of the sniggering faces at the station, she would give the middle finger. And she heard it tickled people these days whenever a woman said suck my dick. All in all, life outside the spotlight didn't seem so bad. Hell, Chief Fenwick probably had the right idea.

There was only freedom out there for her now, and that included for tonight. Once she was done eating, she would shower and then hit the sheets. A tiny doze of Dark Ether, and she would be up in the high heavens. The plastic bag crinkled in her pocket with every slight shift in her seat.

To think all it had taken was Frank tripping to introduce her to this wonder. They had been together in his lab, and he had been analyzing a sample of the substance for the umpteenth time. Something about wanting to photograph its microscopic structure for clues to where D.E got his. And oddly placed stool, and he was tumbling with a large cache of the drug spilling onto her face. There had been the freak out when she passed out.

He thought she would die that all he had done was try to revive her using first aid with the ingredients present in the lab. He almost shed a tear when she eventually came to.

Days after the incident, Jessica realized she wanted more Dark Ether. She had tried to fight it off at first. Then one day, it turned up at the dinner table. She had only suggested it one time as a joke, but Frank's pliability sometimes popped up in the weirdest places.

Sex had been mind blowing that night. And then they had gone on using for a while before Frank forced a clampdown. It wasn't meant to be a habit, and it was totally inappropriate. Jessica agreed with him, and they called it quits with the drug.

She had been serious. But it was hard to not introduce it to James during one of their plays and so, it had gone on and on. There was a certain rigidity to how most of the world saw things. Sometimes, what was called the wrong choice was only just an alternative choice.

Everything had it risks, and only a few people got it.
Her meal done, Jessica blew out the candles and moved into the kitchen. She got down to loading the dishes into the dishwasher. She was too dazed and happy to realize she was being watched.

"Here you go," James said, handing Frank a glass of bourbon. He had thrown a shirt on and was a little stiff as he took a seat opposite Frank. "Go on, let it out. What were you blubbering about? You said you were on to the Dark Ether?"

Frank scoffed, smiling a bitter smile as he took a sip of his liquor.
"On to him? I found the bastard. Met him."
James leaned forwards in his seat. "You can't be serious."
"Oh, I am. I am quite alright. You see, I had a sense. A hunch."
"Go on. Spit it out. What hunch?" James said. He was getting impatient.

"Black hair," Frank said. "My God, it was staring us in the face the whole time. Did you ever take a close look at those two new victims? Did they strike you as familiar?"
"Familiar? What are you talking about?"

"Obsessed. The motherfucker's obsessed," Frank said. "All over the walls. His mind—I had to pretend to—"
"Come on now, I can't make heads or tails of what you're saying. What's the point to all this?" James barked.

"The point?" Frank pulled out a gun and aimed it at James's chest. James paused. He glanced down at the gun and tried to play it cool. "What the hell is this about?"
"You know what it's about," Frank said, mirthlessly. "You suspected. That's why you threw a shirt on, to conceal the fact that you're now carrying a gun."

"Right." James leaned back into his seat. "And I'm guessing the yarn about leaving town was all part of the cover up. How do you plan on going about it all?"

"Is this the part where you try to distract me by getting me to talk of my plan, until you get the drop on me? You must be out of you mind. I'm sure Jess must have mentioned my focusing abilities. Women talk about such things, however inappropriate. But yes. It does involve something I've been planning for a while just in case. You're just an improve piece right now."

"Mhmm," James said. "So the bit about going undercover and finding Dark Ether was all hooey then?"
"You know this already. Still trying to stall?" Frank said, smiling. "You'd have to be from the wild west to outgun me at this range. I didn't have to find Dark Ether.

I knew him all along. He was me."
"He was—" James froze. Everything but his eyes which roved about went stiff as he tried to piece things together. Slowly, his eyes came back to rest on Frank as realization set in.

"Yes," Frank said, nodding. "These women. They make you do the craziest things. One's got to vent one way or the other. You'd know this if you'd ever gotten married. Instead you went about fucking other people's wives."

"Now wait a minute—"
"Nuhuh," Frank shushed him. "You're all out of lines in this story, James. I just have one question, did you ever laugh? When you saw me running around the precinct, chasing after Jess's coattails, did you laugh?"

"I didn't, Frank," James said. He was shaking visibly now. "It was—"
"I told you you were all out of lines, Mr. Reeves," Frank told him, strengthening his gun arm. "I'll have fun fucking your corpse when you're gone. Now, stay still."

"No." James tried to jump away.
Bang! The shot blasted a big pit of red on his chest. Bang! Bang! Frank fired two more for good measure.

He rose carefully from his seat. Like the car currently waiting in a garage somewhere to drive him straight out of town for the flight back to Ohio, Frank had a burner phone within which would be discovered James's plans and discussions with a confederate in their shared identity as Dark Ether. His work here was done.

Odds and Ends

The key. The key. The Bible was the key. He had tried to tell her before, but she wouldn't listen. Now, there would be no one to stop him as he entered.

His heart thump-thump-thumped in his chest. The key had worked. The key worked and he was in. His face felt hot with the heat of his breath as the mask threw it back at him, but it didn't matter. Visibility was perfect. This was the biggest high he had ever had in his entire life.

He was sweaty all over. His dick swelled in his pants. He had the urge to right it, but there was Dark Ether taped to his hands. All he had to do was grab her. All he had to do was sneak up on her and grab her. That didn't seem like a big problem. He had seen her dance her way into the kitchen. She had airpods on. Just a quick grab, and it would be over.

Fuck, shit, fuck. He didn't think he could do it. He didn't think he would be able to hold it off long enough to get inside her before blowing his wad. God, the tension was killing him. And why did he suddenly feel all so scratchy?

He made his way through the hallway towards the kitchen. There she was. With her ass bent over and wiggling as she tried to take something out of the washer, she seemed to be inviting him, egging him on. He swallowed the lump in his throat and took the step forward.

He didn't know what it was, perhaps a roach, perhaps something else, but she was straightening up when she yelped all of a sudden and whirled around to face him. Fuck, shit, fuck. It was his reflection in the window. He had forgotten all about the window.

They stared at each other for four long seconds. The height, the sneak, the whorls on his mask, he was here. He was in her house. Dark Ether was in her house. And he had come for her. This shit is surreal, she thought as the first shudders hit her.

She was trembling. She was scared of him. She was trembling because she was scared on him. This sent a jolt of energy coursing through him that he couldn't help snarling. He saw her look sideways and followed her eyes to the knife rack. Oh, shit, it was on. Any second now. She took the steps and he lunged at her.

He bulled into her and knocked her over even as her fingers grasped the knife rack. The entire thing came cascading on them as they both slid to the ground. They were struggling, both of them huffing.

"Ahp, get off—" Jessica said, gasping for air even as her fingers tried to grasp at anything in particular. She felt a handle and held on to it. She slashed down at him and saw she had used the unsharpened side. "You bitch!" he yelled as he knocked the knife aside. He whipped a backhand slap to her face.

The blow knocked her aside but brought her attention to the reddish darkness of his palms. Dark ether. He had dark ether, but he hadn't yet used it on her. She was still good. Quickly, she grabbed at his palms, trying to hold them off as she screamed.

"Helllp!"
The sound came from the kitchen. It had begun. The Father had brought judgment and it was happening in the kitchen and it had begun. Matthew hurried back from the bedroom and headed towards the kitchen.

"Helllp!" she screamed some more.
The bitch was like a tiger, a viper, a snake, he thought as he struggled to keep her down.He could see all his dark ether wasting off, wiping away on her arms as he tried to force her arms down. This bitch was something else.

"Helllllp!" she screamed again.
He grabbed her stiffly by the shoulder—"Stay down, bitch!"—and slammed her hard back on the floor. It was so hard he felt the wind go out of her with a groan.

"Ughh," he groaned. Was she good? Was she dead? She wasn't supposed to—
He heard a sound behind him. A chuckle.
"Babylon the Great!"
"What the—" he grabbed the thing closest to him and moved in quick.

There was no resistance as the knife slid right into Matthew's belly. He looked amused first, then horrified as he glanced down at the knife.

What the hell? The boy? How did this—what the—wasn't he—
"Fuck!" Fred yelled as he pulled the knife out and rolled up his mask. "Nononono," he said as he caught the boy and let him down slowly. This wasn't supposed to happen. This wasn't how it was supposed to be.

Her head was woozy and her vision swam. Both the ceiling and the floor beneath her seemed to wobble and shift. When Jessica turned her head, there was Matthew lying down on the floor with his face turned to her, and Dark Ether was kneeling over him. What was goin—

She groaned as a headache wooshed in. Dark Ether turned to her. "You bitch!" he said as he hurried over and slapped her. Through the haze of it all, she realized there was something wrong with his face. He seemed—he looked—was he Fred?

Jessica's eyes shone in horror all of a sudden. "Fred!"
***
"Yeah, you fucking whore," Fred said, holding the bloody knife to her throat. "It's me alright. Look what you've done. Look what you've done."

He pointed the knife at the boy's body. All movement had ceased. He turned back to face Jessica.

"I'm going to take my time in enjoying every fucking minute of your humiliation."

He slid the knife through she shirt, ripping it wide open, with her breasts exposed to all the world. Dark areolas. They made his penis jump.

He was growling like a rabid dog, his mouth watering for effect as his hands rode down to her yoga pants. He heard footsteps beside him and turned. It was Frank with a gun aimed dead at him.
"Hey."
Bang!

The shot whipped Fred off her with such force that it woke her up. She jumped upright, shrieking, clutching her blouse to herself as she shifted backwards on the floor.

Fred didn't even stir one bit.
Frank hurried over to her while she howled and pulled her close to him. She was a shuddering wreck while he soothed her.
"Hey, there there. It's okay now. Calm down. Calm—" he froze. She looked up to find him staring at Matthew's body.
"No," he said. "How the… No."

He hurried over to Matthew cradling him. "Nonononono," he said. "My son. How in the world? My son. I'm sorry, Matthew. I'm sorry." Jessica sat there, shaking, staring at him. There was something about this which didn't feel—my son. My son. The Father. What was that? She didn't quite understand it yet.

He began to stroke Matthew's hair, and that was when Jessica saw them. His gloves. They were latex gloves, work gloves. How did he know to put them on? The Father.

Her phone started vibrating on the floor where it had tumbled during the struggle, startling them both. That was something else. Hadn't he—

"Hey, Frank," she said, sticking a hand into her pocket. "When did you get back? Didn't you call me from Georgia earlier this afternoon?"

Frank stiffened. Then he relaxed as he set his boy down on the ground. He turned and crawled over to her. She could see from his face that he was struggling to get his emotions under control.

"Hi, umm… how are you?" he said, not quite looking at her. She chuckled. "Me? I'm a whore. That's what he called me. Just out of curiosity, if he thought I was Babylon the Great, who did he call 'The Father'? the Father who brings judgment."

A pause hung between them. She saw him go stiff, his muscles tensing up for the attack.Ready? He exploded with both arms reaching for her throat when she slammed a palm full of dark ether into his face. He froze, confused as some of hit flew straight into his nose.

There was no pause for her, and he couldn't stop her as she grabbed hold of the bloody knife and, screaming, sank it straight home into his throat.

She tipped him over, choking, gurgling on his own blood, knife sticking out of his neck. She crawled away from him and grabbed her phone. It was the precinct.

There were three men dead or dying in her house. She couldn't yet make out the full details of precisely what had happened, so when she answered, she told them the least exciting thing about it all. "I've got Dark Ether in my house."

COMING SOON!!!!!

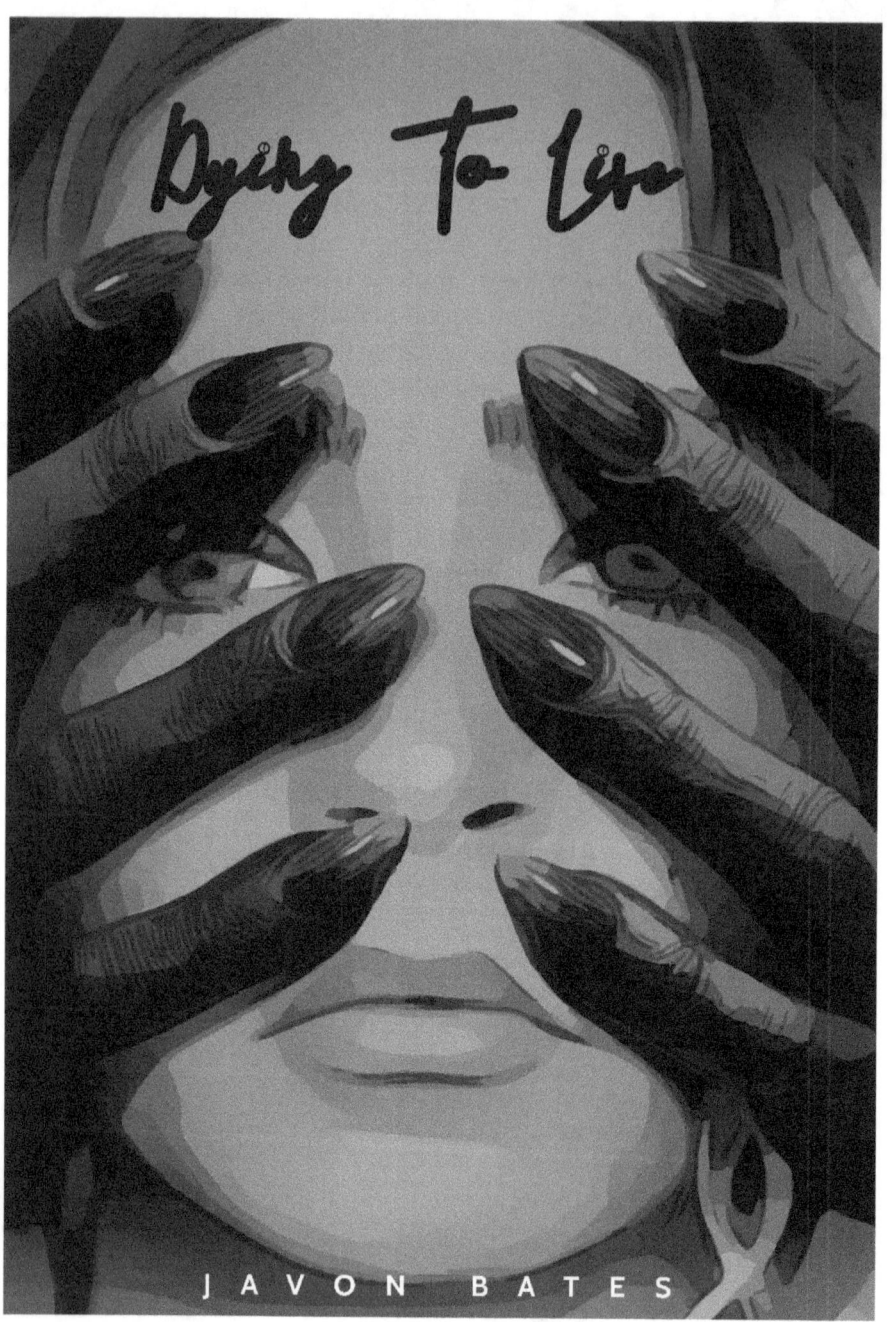